The Summons

Brittiany West

This is a work of fiction. All characters and events portrayed in this book are fictitious.

THE SUMMONS

2012 © by Brittiany West

Cover design by Brittiany West

For Beej, for helping me bring Lily to life

Chapter One

I heard the distant waves before I opened my eyes. The streets remained quiet; most people didn't get up until around ten or so. Usually, I slept in, but I couldn't sleep today. I'd looked forward to this day for more than two years. The surf practically called my name, luring me with the promise of perfect, smooth breakers and turbulent swells. My surfboard stood in the corner, covered in new wax and ready to go. But why had I even bothered? I wouldn't be able to go.

"Lily?"

I jumped out of bed quickly, something I never did before when mom called my name. I used to fake sleep or pretend I couldn't hear her so I could get a few more winks. But things were different now.

I rushed from my small bedroom, banging my arms against the closed-in walls of the hallway. Unlike most apartments in the slums, mom kept ours neat and clean. Other places stayed shabby and rundown, with rats crawling through the mottled walls. As soon as we moved in, mom went to work patching, scrubbing and sanitizing until the place gleamed.

"Yeah, mom? Are you ok?" My stomach dropped as I noticed deep purple shadows under her eyes. The night took its toll on her. She sat in the small recliner, watching the news. The reporter went on and on about more disappearances.

"I'm fine, honey." She fixed me with that penetrating glare that always made me nervous. I racked my brains, trying to think of something I might have done in the past few days to get in trouble. "I'm just worried about you."

"Why?" I shrugged, hoping I looked casual. "I'm fine."

She frowned in a motherly sort of way. "Today is the big senior beach trip, isn't it?"

How did she always know these things? I'd been so careful to keep quiet about it. "Yeah, but I don't really want to go."

"Lily, you've been talking about this trip ever since you got into high school. Cherie and Crystal will miss you if you don't go."

"Mom, it's really no big deal." I walked to the kitchen and rummaged in the cupboard for some cereal.

"I know why you're not going," she pressed. "And I won't have it."

"Mom, I'm not leaving you alone here, ok?" My voice rose louder than I'd meant it to. "I just…I just don't want anything to happen."

"The cancer hasn't gotten the better of me yet." My stomach clenched at the sound of that word coming from her lips. "I want you to have fun, and enjoy your last few days of high school instead of worrying about me all the time."

"Mom…"

"I'm not arguing with you, Lily. You're going, and that's final."

Her lips set themselves in a firm line. She'd made up her mind about it now. Mom always tried to let me make my own choices, but occasionally she wore the deadpan expression that made it clear I was not allowed to argue. Resignedly, I finished my cereal, put on one of my swimsuits and meandered moodily through the door.

My hunched shoulders finally relaxed and my breath came a little easier as I pulled away from the city onto the main highway to the beach. The warm, salt-scented air seemed to have a healing effect on me. No matter how bad things got, a few hours surfing always helped me cope. I often wished that we could move to the beach cliff property where the air felt cleaner, but our limited income wouldn't even begin to cover it.

Even though the party technically started at nine, hardly any people sat on the beach when I pulled up. I laid down my towel and surfboard on a spot close to shore and stretched out to think. My mind jumbled trying to remember all the medicines I needed to pick up for mom, tests I needed to take before the end of the year and homework that still needed finished before Monday. I rubbed my eyes tiredly and rolled over to feel the sun on my back.

"You're up early," said a mocking voice above me. I sat up to see Cherie standing next to me with my other best friend, Crystal. They tossed their boards and towels down next to me.

"Haha," I muttered. I didn't pay them much attention as I looked out at the water curling against the shore. I'd watched the forecast last night, depressed at the thought of missing the promised swells. But now that mom forced me to go, I wouldn't let the waves go to waste. I picked up my board and walked closer to the shore. The sand felt pleasantly warm under my feet, not freezing, not scorching. As if on cue, the ocean grew steadily more turbulent. Perfect.

"You two in?" I turned to Cherie and Crystal, who shook their heads at once.

"I came to tan and check out hot guys, not look like a drowned rat," said Crystal as she untied her perfect, curly blonde hair and shook it out.

"I'll be out in a bit," said Cherie. "I need to sunscreen first." She pulled out a massive bottle of SPF 50 and carefully squeezed out a tiny, perfect puddle into her palm. Of course. Cherie's sunscreen ritual would take a good twenty minutes at least, and the waves would die by then.

"Why did you guys even bring your boards?" I scoffed. Without waiting for an answer, I turned and ran towards the waves, my feet slapping against the wet sand near the shore.

I hit every single wave I went for. The water seemed to rise and bend to my will, knowing my every move. The sun shone down on the water as I paddled through and coasted down the waves.

After a while, I sat up on my board and took a break to tie my hair up. I looked back to the beach, scanning for Cherie and Crystal when I noticed something odd. A boy, Wes Landon, stared at me from the shore. I casually looked behind me, but I couldn't see anyone nearby. Did he watch me surf the whole time?

A strange curiosity rose inside me. I knew Wes. We'd gone to school together all these years, passed each other a million times in the hallways, but we hadn't ever talked. Our groups didn't mix, and I'd never really thought about him before. We'd shared one freshman biology class, but we sat across the room from each other. Why did he focus on me now?

Feeling a little unnerved, I shrugged it off and searched for my board. I pulled it towards me through the water by the ankle leash and jogged towards the shore.

"See any good specimens yet?" I asked Crystal as I plopped down next to her on my towel. She smirked.

"Some. The rest of the seniors are finally here."

"Speaking of which," said Cherie, dabbing sunscreen on her feet, "I noticed Wes Landon couldn't keep his eyes off of you."

"Whatever," I replied, rolling my eyes. "Aren't you done yet? I was in the water at least twenty minutes."

"We were debating whether Wes is digging on you," said Crystal. She lifted her sunglasses and wagged her eyebrows at me. "That's why it took so long."

"He doesn't like me. He was probably just checking out the waves."

"More like who was *in* the waves!" Crystal shrieked as I threw a handful of sand at her.

"I don't have time for that crap," I shot back. And honestly, I didn't. Between school and mom, I pretty much had no social life at all, minus hanging out with the two Cs.

"You're just saying that because of Dave," Cherie put in with a grin. "Not every guy is going to break your heart like he did. Love always strikes when you least expect it."

"Well, it'll just have to wait," I muttered darkly. I threw a handful of sand at Cherie too, for good measure. "I'm going to go get a hamburger. You guys want anything?"

"No," they replied in unison.

I shouldn't have even been thinking of lunch at this hour, but in my desperation for a distraction I didn't really care. Most of the seniors at Dean High School showed up for the party, but only a few people gathered around the large grill where the gym teacher, Coach Green, flipped burgers and turned hot dogs. I got in line and grabbed a plain burger with cheese.

"No ketchup?" said a voice behind me. "Not even a little tomato or anything?"

I turned around to see Wes standing there, smiling down at me flirtatiously. I'd never really stood close to him before. I noticed his eyes were an oddly beautiful shade of hazel. With his curly brown hair and round chin, he looked almost boyish instead of a senior in high school.

"I don't really like anything on my hamburger but cheese." I sounded prudish even to myself, but that weird feeling of intimidated interest washed over me again, making it hard to talk normally. Wes shrugged, his smile not wavering at all.

"Well, you don't know what you're missing." He gestured to his burger loaded with everything from pickles to mayonnaise. "That's a real burger."

"Whatever floats your boat," I replied, rolling my eyes at him. I didn't know why, but I didn't want to talk to him. I walked away, not bothering to smile back.

"I saw you surfing today," he said. He followed me with a strange kind of insistence.

"Good for you. Are you stalking me or something?" He ignored the comment and kept walking, keeping pace with my faster steps.

"Just finding you interesting," he replied. "Is that ok with you?"

"Not really." I couldn't help but notice he didn't gawk at me like most guys did. He kept his eyes on my eyes, a genuinely interested expression on his face. No one ever looked at me so directly and honestly before, and it caught me off guard.

"Ok, ok, I can take a hint." His eyes lingered again on mine for a minute before he turned away and walked back towards his friends. I stood still for a moment, trying to process what I felt. I didn't really feel mad at him, just indifferent. And yet...

I turned around resolutely before my thoughts could wander into dangerous territory. Cherie and Crystal grinned before I even got close.

"So...what did he say?"

"Just goofing around, nothing important," I said. "Trust me, nothing will ever happen with me and Wes Landon."

We spent the rest of the day lounging in the sun, scrutinizing all the gorgeous, god-like surfers and making fun of the bimbo cheerleaders while we ate chips and drank pop. Everyone started filtering towards the parking lot when the sun began to dip towards the horizon. Some good swells started to rise again, and most people got out of the water.

"I'm gonna go catch a few waves," I told Cherie and Crystal. "Wanna come?"

Cherie's eyes narrowed with worry. "It looks a bit rough out there, don't you think?"

"No. It's fine. Come if you want to."

With that, I ran out and jumped on my board. The water felt pleasantly cold after the heat of the day. Goosebumps rippled up my legs and arms as I paddled. My arms ached by the time I got out to the deep, but I kept pushing myself into the huge wave headed for me.

The powerful wall of water caught me off guard. It moved faster than anything I'd ever done before. I popped up, nearly losing my footing, then relaxed as the adrenaline set in. I coasted down the wave easily, just like I'd done with all the others that morning. My confidence soared. I'd never seen anyone take a wave like this, much less done it myself.

I stepped back on my board a bit, then felt a roaring wave of panic sweep through my stomach as I slipped over the edge. I landed on the curl of the water with a loud smack and turned over and over, spitting salt out of my mouth. Vertigo made my stomach turn as I plunged deeper into the water. The undertow grasped at me, pulling me like a large hand down, down to the darkness. I struggled desperately until my body felt rigid with fear and exhaustion. I couldn't see, I couldn't move. Heavy, dark water closed over me with suffocating pressure as I tried to draw my last breath.

Chapter Two

Suddenly, I felt strong arms wrap around my body and pull me up. I opened my eyes, cringing as the salt stung them. I could barely see a tan face surrounded by curly brown hair. I put my arms around my rescuer and closed my eyes again.

We reached the surface and I gasped for air like a dying fish. My eyes blurred as I tried to blink the water out. Someone removed my leash and cradled me.

"Is she ok?" said a frantic voice.

"She's fine, just give her air."

I felt him put me gently on the sand. His hand rested on my cheek.

"Lily, can you hear me?"

I rubbed my face and looked up. Wes came into focus above me, his hazel eyes full of panic.

"You must be crazy to go out there in a swell like this," he said, looking relieved.

I knew I should have been grateful, but I felt stupid and awkward for nearly drowning in front of Wes. I sat up abruptly, turning away from his touch.

"Thanks," I said stiffly. Crystal knelt nearby in the sand, looking torn between fear and a fit of giggles. Wes took my hand firmly and helped me stand up. Even through my indignation, a tingling wave of chills swept over me from his firm but gentle touch. I pulled my hand away and brushed it against my wet shorts, trying to forget the electrifying feeling he'd given me.

"I need to get going," I said, looking at Crystal and Cherie and purposely avoiding Wes's stare. They looked at each other and rolled their eyes simultaneously. "See you on Monday."

I gathered up my towel and board, which Wes must have gotten from the water, and ran for my car.

"Lily!"

He followed me and I sped up, hoping to hop in the front seat before he could catch up. As I grabbed my door handle, he reached for my arm. The same intense wave of chills washed over me, freezing me from my toes to my hair. *What's my problem? I don't even know this guy.* I wrinkled my nose in disgust, irritated that he could have such an effect on me.

"What?" I demanded.

"I just…wanted to make sure you were ok." His face fell, revealing just how hurt he really felt. I felt a small stab of guilt. "I thought it was weird. I mean, you didn't even cough up any water or anything."

He quickly moved his hand away from my arm and bit his lip. He looked more like a little boy than ever.

"I'm all right," I replied, my voice heavy with a sudden exhaustion. "I need to get home."

"Can I drive you?"

"I can't just leave my car here. The night beach bums would have a heyday," I replied. "Thanks, though."

"I can drive with you and walk home after," he offered. "I'm not trying to be a stalker, I promise I just want to make sure you're ok. I don't know about you, but I probably wouldn't want to drive after nearly drowning."

He fixed me with that stare of his, an almost pleading look in his eyes. "What about your car?" I asked him slowly.

"Didn't drive," he replied. "I live close to the beach."

"Oh." A fierce battle raged in my brain. After what I'd said, I couldn't ask him to take me home. But a small part of me wanted badly to be with him, to feel his protective arms around my shoulders, reassuring me. I pushed the feeling down, snuffed it out.

"Um…no, I'm all right," I finally said. "I don't live that close to the beach, and you'd probably have a long walk. Thanks again." That, and I knew he'd probably freak out about my neighborhood. But then again, why would I care what he thought?

"Suit yourself." He shrugged, trying to look indifferent, but I could tell he still hurt. "See you at school."

He walked away, leaving me feeling unsettled and awkward. I climbed into the driver's side and started the car. As I pulled slowly out of the beach parking lot, a surge of regret swept through me. Maybe it would have been nice to have him with me after all.

I wound through the darkening streets, trying to hurry before the thugs started wandering the sidewalks. Shady-looking people were already out and about, trading cigarettes and digging in trash cans. I pulled into the parking garage, parked and hurried up the steps.

"Hi honey," said mom as I shut the door and put the bolts in place. "Did you have fun?"

"What?" I looked up to see a small smile playing across her lips.

"You met a boy, didn't you?"

I rearranged my face into a scowl. "No," I replied. "What makes you say that?"

"Your old mom's been around the block, my dear," she said knowingly. "I gave birth to you. I can tell when you're flustered about a boy."

"Mom, gag! I didn't meet a boy, I just had a weird day."

She smirked. "And…you put your keys in the trash can when you came in."

"No, I didn't." I looked down into the trash can my mom always kept between the couch and the front door. Sure enough, my keys laid there on a stack of junk mail.

"Oh," I stooped down to pick them up. "Well, I'm just tired. I had a bit of trouble surfing."

"What happened?" she asked, her voice rising with concern.

"No big deal, mom, I just fell off my board on a big wave."

"Lily!" She gave a huge, exaggerated sigh. "We've been through this before. I don't want you surfing anymore!"

It never stopped amazing me how she jumped from one emotion to the next so fluidly. One minute, she's cool mom talking about boys, the next, overprotecting mamma bear. I sighed. I'd heard this lecture so many times that I mouthed it to myself while she said it out loud.

"Sharks aren't afraid to bite, Lily, you know that. Scientists have shown that some sharks do attack randomly! Not to mention jellyfish, or drowning, or the tide. You could end up lost at sea. You're my only daughter, and I'm not losing you to something as silly as…"

I drifted in and out of awareness, catching snippets here and there about too much sun exposure and on and on. I wanted desperately to escape to my room.

"Mom, I'm fine," I cut her off. "I've had accidents before and survived. And besides, Wes…"

I stopped short, but it was too late. A wide grin spread across mom's face, lightening the shadows under her eyes.

"Wes, huh? What a studly name." And now back to the cool mom.

"Well…he's not," I said shortly. I got enough of this dumbness from Cherie and Crystal. I definitely didn't need it from mom. Didn't she realize she's so much more important than some guy?

"Did he rescue you? Was it terribly romantic?"

"Mom!"

"I'm just teasing you, honey," she laughed. "Let me have a bit of fun, will you?"

I plopped down in the other chair and put my feet up on the coffee table, munching on the bowl of cereal I had just poured for myself.

"Do you eat anything but cereal?" she asked.

"Mmm…no." I smiled. "Did you get some dinner? Can I get you anything?"

"Yeah, I had some soup before you got home," she replied. "Thanks for asking. You take such good care of me, sweetie."

"Oh, mom." Luckily, she turned back to the TV and didn't see the tears forming in my eyes.

Chapter Three

Monday dawned with stormy clouds and a slight drizzle, a stark contrast to the sunshine over the weekend. I leaned forward and rested my head on my steering wheel after I finally found a parking spot at school. My eyes burned with weariness. Mom's midnight pain, along with strange dreams about running through trees, kept me up most of the night. With a heavy sigh, I grabbed my books and sauntered to the front gates.

A huge line waited for me as I stepped up to the metal detectors. I couldn't help but feel a little like cattle every time I stood in this line, waiting to get our bags run through the See-thru scan. A couple kids felt the same way I did, judging by the way they made mooing noises at the proctors.

People whispered all around me, looking a little panicked. I stood on tiptoe to see what everyone talked about. A guy in uniform stood up near the gates, peering closely at everyone who passed through. The black uniform came with a stiff cap, the shoulders trimmed with red tassels. Why would the school send someone from the Mainframe? Government officials only came on career day or during the semi-annual propaganda speech. It definitely explained why the line stretched so long. Nobody wanted to pass him.

My turn came. Nervously, I set my bag on the conveyer belt. The Mainframe man looked over at me. He'd given most of the other kids a second of scrutiny before turning back to face the crowd, but he rested his eyes on me much longer than the others. A huge lump formed in my throat. I forced it down, trying not to betray my nerves. His eyebrows arched slowly in a look of surprise as he eyed the mandatory barcode name tag pinned to my sweater. The stare didn't last long, though. He quickly pushed his eyebrows back down into the same hard scowl he gave everyone else. *He looks like he's found what he's looking for.* The thought crossed my mind so randomly, making me feel unsettled and a little scared. No. It couldn't be.

I grabbed my bag and raced through the gate as soon as it cleared, trying not to shout with impatience while another proctor scanned my nametag for attendance. She finished and I hurried away. I chanced a glance over my shoulder and saw the Mainframe man still looking at me, a satisfied smirk playing about his lips. I shivered and forced myself not to run to Cherie and Crystal.

"Hey, where were you? The bell's about to ring," said Cherie as I walked up. They waited in the usual spot at the front doors.

"I uh…had some trouble with mom," I replied, trying to sound nonchalant. For some reason, I didn't want to tell them about the creepy man at the gate.

"Oh." Only Cherie and Crystal knew about mom. I couldn't bear the sympathetic stares and the muttering in the hallways, so I didn't tell anyone.

"Well, come on, let's go watch Miss Tanners take flight with her flappy arms," said Crystal.

I felt a warm surge of gratitude for my friends. They always knew how to make me laugh. We always started the day with Chem. Our teacher, Miss Tanners, looked about a hundred years old. She had flab on her arms that hung down way farther than typical arm flab. Whenever she typed on the giant black-screen, the flaps of skin waved back and forth, making her look like some weird bird about to take off. Sometimes we counted her down and tried not to explode into fits of giggles when she flapped faster with each count. I knew we shouldn't make fun of her, but I couldn't help it. Laughs were hard to come by these days.

"Why was that guy here?" asked Crystal. She looked nervous too. Had the man stared at her like he'd stared at me?

"I don't know. Let's just get to Chem," I said quickly.

Unfortunately, a sallow-looking guy in his mid-twenties sat in Miss Tanner's chair. Great. A sub. He couldn't have looked unhappier to be there, and he didn't even write his name on the board.

"I'd give you a 'Good morning,' but it's not a particularly good one," he said in a bored voice. "I don't want to be here, you don't want to be here, so just turn in whatever you're supposed to turn in and get on with the assignment on the board. If you need help, ask your parents when you get home."

What a jerk. I looked at him disgustedly as he buried himself in a book. Why become a teacher if you hate kids? His hair hung in greasy dreds around his huge ears, but I noticed his skin most of all. I'd never seen skin so pale. His eyes flashed strangely, making him look even more sour and angry. He could probably cut through someone by just looking at them. An unpleasant shiver crept up my spine.

He looked up suddenly and stared at me. Startled, I forced my eyes back down to my blank piece of paper. He knew I'd been watching him. I felt a weird sort of terror about him, but I didn't really know why.

I grabbed a pencil and scribbled a quick note to Crystal:

Is it just me, or does that guy majorly creep you out?

A few minutes later, she wrote back and stealthily sent it my way:

Yeah, he does. What's his deal anyway?

I scrawled a quick note back and shoved it on her desk right before the creepy sub looked up:

I don't know…he seems sick or something.

Crystal was in the middle of writing her reply when a note from Cherie suddenly appeared on my desk:

This guy is seriously scary.

Before long, notes circulated between the three of us until one got snatched out of my hands mid-sentence. I looked up in horror to see the evil sub reading the note with increasingly narrowed eyes. I swallowed hard.

"Writing notes, are we?" he asked, looking coldly down at me. I figured it wouldn't do any good to lie, so I just shrugged.

"Sorry, sir."

"Perhaps you should spend some time in study hall since you can't seem to contain yourself in class." He thrust a hall pass at me. I tried not to gag as I noticed long, crusty, yellow fingernails on his hands.

Study hall at Dean High School wasn't like study hall used to be. You had to sit in a room where teachers sent students they couldn't handle, kind of like mid-day detention. Since the principal only cared about getting a district level job, he'd come up with Study Hall as a solution for disgruntled teachers. Some gym coach was always in there on the off period, supposedly monitoring students, but usually just watching sports on a communicator. The dregs of the school were always there too, smoking or flashing their pocket knives threateningly.

I stood up slowly, feeling a ripple of anger at the pitying looks from Cherie and Crystal. They'd been writing notes too and hadn't gotten in trouble. I grabbed my backpack and stomped through the door into the hallway. I stopped at a drinking fountain and took a long drink.

"Skipping class?"

I jumped, startled, and sent a spray of water all over my shirt. Wes stood behind me, a sly smile on his face.

"I got sent to Study Hall," I replied, angrily wiping water off of my face and top. "What's your excuse?"

"Student body official business." I remembered suddenly that he'd been voted class treasurer.

"On the third to last day of school?" I scoffed. He caught me staring at the pop in his hands.

"Ok, so I took a side trip to the vending machine. But at least I didn't get sent to Study Hall."

"Did you follow me just to torment me?"

He playfully punched my arm. "Hey, relax a little, I'm just teasing." His eyes softened slightly as he once again fixed them on mine. "You want some company?"

"In Study Hall?"

He shrugged. "I know it can be a pain. It might be a little more bearable with a friend. Besides, I don't think Coach-whoever will even notice."

My heart beat slightly faster. A friend? I shook myself slightly and pushed the thought hard from my mind.

"Since when did we become friends?" I sounded harsh, but I couldn't help it. Boys were out of the question right now.

"Since now," he shot back. He put his hand on my shoulder and turned me to face him. "Why are you so afraid to get to know me? Do I smell or something? I *do* shower. I mean, most days."

I laughed before I could catch myself, surprised by how good it felt. As much as I didn't want to admit it, I realized that being with Wes felt comfortable, uncomplicated. I acted completely differently around him than I did with other guys, always self-conscious and out of place. I didn't hide the real me under a façade of shallow flirtatiousness.

"I'm not afraid," I muttered. "I'm just too busy for boys right now."

"Whoa, whoa, whoa…I didn't ask you out! I just want to hang out, get to know you better. Is that such a crime?"

Before I could say something back, the door to Miss Tanners' class opened and the evil sub's head shot out. He looked straight at me, completely shocking me. He didn't look like some random sub, annoyed with babysitting teenagers all day. He looked at me with pure hatred etched over every feature of his sallow face. His eyes narrowed maliciously as he left the room and walked down the hall.

Chapter Four

"I thought I told you to get to Study Hall," he hissed. Is this how subs normally act? I dug in my memory for some other sub who acted this vindictively, but none came close to this guy. I stepped back, unconsciously looking for a weapon.

"We're just going, sir." Wes looked a little scared, but he stood up straight, his fists clenched. "I'll make sure she gets there."

The sub stared angrily at me a few seconds longer, then turned and went back in the room without another word. I let out a breath I didn't know I'd been holding.

"Man, what a creep." Wes looked at me. "He's…not normal."

I tried to push down the fear that crept up inside me. Two creepy people in one day? What are the odds?

Without replying, I turned around and walked as quickly as I could to Study Hall. Wes followed, and soon we stepped into the room and took two desks in the back. I recognized Coach Benson, the basketball coach, sitting at the desk up front. He didn't even look up when we came in. I heard the sounds of a baseball game on his communicator. I scanned the room and breathed a sigh of relief. The crowd wasn't too scary today.

"So you never did answer my question," Wes whispered beside me. I looked around to see him sitting with that casual smile on his face.

"What, about being friends?" He shrugged and ran a hand distractedly through his curly hair. *He's nervous*. The thought unsettled me.

"Yeah."

I considered him for a moment. "All right, fine, we can be friends. But does this mean you'll be stalking me even more? Because I might move if you do."

"I don't know what you're talking about," he said airily, a wide grin spreading across his face. I rolled my eyes, but I couldn't stop myself from smiling a little. It couldn't hurt to be friends as long as nothing else happened. We sat silently for a while as Wes tried to see who was playing on Coach Benson's communicator. I checked the weather on my own communicator.

"You know," he whispered, leaning over, "since we're friends now, I'm completely entitled to let you know about Ted Jones's graduation party next Friday night. Interested?"

I looked at him, feeling guarded again. "Are you asking me on a date?"

"You said it, not me," he replied with a grin. "But I don't have to pick you up if you don't want me to. We can arrive completely separate if you'd like. I just thought I'd be a good friend and let you know about it."

I stared down at my nails, debating. It was slightly surreal, talking about some party. My world had been so torn apart that I'd almost forgotten what it felt like to just a be a normal teenager. Crystal and Cherie and I still hung out pretty regularly, but I hadn't been to an actual party since the beginning of my sophomore year.

"I...I don't know," I replied slowly. "Doesn't he live in a pretty rich neighborhood?"

"All the better! And besides, it's not like they're going to be checking social status at the door."

"Well...I might be there, I might not. It just depends."

"On what?"

"Just on whether I'm busy or not," I said, evading his stare even more.

"Ok, ok, hint taken again." He held his hands up in mock surrender. The bell rang and I quickly gathered up my things before Wes could see the blush creeping up my cheeks.

I passed through the usual zoo exhibit in the hallway. Everyone seemed even more restless now with the onset of summer. People didn't want to sit and listen when we could be out surfing or boating or hanging out at the boardwalk. Several people, mostly seniors, took advantage of the weather anyway and skipped school.

I walked into English class and took my usual desk between Crystal and Cherie. Mrs. Thomas walked up and down the aisles, collecting the last big essay of the year. Mrs. Thomas loved my compositions, a well-known fact. I couldn't help but grin with pride when she took my paper and smiled.

"'The Road not Taken, by Robert Frost: A Comparison of Life and Literature,'" she read aloud. "Sounds like another great piece, Lily. I think your professors will be impressed next year."

"Thank you, Mrs. Thomas," I replied, my heart dropping. I'd gotten a scholarship to go to the college in Parthin, but mom's sickness changed all that. I couldn't go off to school when she needed my help.

"You're still planning to major in English, right? I'd hate to see a great writer go to waste."

"I…might," I replied. "I'll probably just get my feet wet first, try a few different subjects and see what I like best."

"Well, think about it anyway," she said cheerfully. I felt a small twinge of guilt. It was a lie of course, but I kept up the story that I was still going away in the fall. Mrs. Thomas first recommended me for the scholarship, and I felt too embarrassed to admit the truth. Her words burned in my mind. English came naturally to me. It would be incredible to study some of the older texts, but I didn't really have a choice. Mom has nobody else.

We spent the rest of the period watching an old movie about *Hamlet*, our last reading assignment, as a reward for finishing our essays. Cherie, Crystal and I spent the rest of the period talking quietly instead of watching.

"What happened with creepy dude while I was in study hall?" I whispered over Hamlet's exaggerated soliloquy.

"He just sat there while we did our work. Most boring period ever!" Crystal whispered back. "How was study hall?"

"Fine, except…" I stopped just in time.

"What? Was it Wes? Was he there?" said Cherie, picking up immediately on my hesitation and correctly interpreting it. It's a pain having friends who can practically read my mind. I couldn't stop the blush from creeping up my neck again, but luckily they didn't see it in the dark room.

"It *was* him! What did he say?" Cherie leaned forward, excited.

"He just acted dumb, as usual," I muttered.

"Oh, come on." Crystal pushed me playfully on the shoulder. "Tell us!"

So I told them about Wes and Ted Jones's party and had to shoosh them before they shrieked.

"He totally invited you the most popular guy in school's party!" Crystal said in a strained whisper. "You have to go!"

"I'm not going anywhere," I replied. "Mom…"

"Lily, I know you're worried about your mom, but she'll be ok for one night." Cherie shrugged. "Besides, this is our last hurrah. Crystal and I are moving a couple days after graduation, and we've got to make the most of the time we have left."

I clenched my teeth, trying to force down the jealousy rising in me. Cherie had purposely left out the fact that they were leaving to go to college in Parthin, without me. The college that I had gotten a scholarship to attend. I knew she didn't want to hurt my feelings, but avoiding the subject hurt more.

"Yeah, but she wouldn't want me at a wild party in an obscenely rich neighborhood." I straightened my papers and put them in my folder.

"Oh, come on, Lily. Tell you what, we'll all go. Spend the night at my house, that way your mom won't worry. The party will be just kind of a...detour," said Crystal with an excited gleam in her eyes.

"Guys, I..."

"Yeah! Come on, no excuses," Cherie agreed. "When did you turn sixty-five? Live a little!"

"I am not sixty-five, I'm just..."

"It's no use, Cherie, she'd rather sit at home and knit like a good girl." Crystal gave a loud, exaggerated sigh and leaned her head on her hand.

"Ok, fine! I'll go to the stupid party!" Both of them really did shriek then, and Mrs. Thomas shooshed them from her desk.

"You guys suck," I whispered under my breath.

"We know," Cherie replied cheerfully. "But you'll thank us later!"

Chapter Five

Graduation day came all too soon. The last week of school passed in a blur. I couldn't help but think every time I walked down the halls that it would be the last time I'd see these teachers, go to these classes and laugh with my friends. For years, this moment seemed unreachable, but it finally came.

I stared at myself in the mirror. I wore the red motorboard cap and gown with the white tassel hanging over my eye. After today, I'd officially be an adult. Or so everyone told me. It used to take forever to grow up, to be able to do the things I wanted to do, but now I longed for childhood, longed to be carefree again.

"I can't believe you're graduating today." I turned around to see mom standing in the bathroom doorway, looking a little misty-eyed. "I know it's not much, but here."

She handed me a small blue box. I opened it to find a beautiful necklace with a delicate silver heart dangling from the chain.

"Mom…its beautiful," I whispered. "But it must have cost a fortune!"

She smiled. "I had some lucky savings. And it's sterling, so it won't turn your skin green."

"Thank you." I put it gently around my neck and closed the clasp. It matched perfectly with the shimmery green dress that I'd gotten for graduation.

An hour later, I sat in a chair in the huge auditorium next to Crystal and Cherie. Wes sat a few rows in front of me. He turned around, caught my eye and winked. I felt a blush creeping up my cheeks, but I did my best to ignore it, and him. Cherie nudged me with her arm and wiggled her eyebrows. I rolled my eyes and stared resolutely at the front of the auditorium.

The principal gave a very long speech that nobody really listened to. People, mostly guys, perked up a little more when Libby Everett gave her speech. They only listened because she's pretty, but I wasn't too impressed. I couldn't figure out how she wound up being top of our class when all she did was party constantly with the other cheerleaders and football players. She rambled on about how we were the future, that we were going to make a difference and change the world. Pretty generic, if you ask me.

Then the principal went through what felt like a thousand names until he got close to mine. He called Wes's name, and the auditorium erupted. Of course. He'd always been popular. He waved jokingly to the crowd, smiling his casual, confident smile.

"You should give him a chance," Crystal whispered. "He's not so bad. *And* he's cute!"

I didn't say anything, but I folded my arms more tightly over my chest. She acted like cute was the only criteria for dating. Yeah, he's cute, but I'd dated so many guys who were just cute and nothing else. If I dated, I wanted to date a man, someone with substance who wouldn't just be a trophy on my arm.

The principal scrolled through a few more names before he finally got to mine. I stood up and made my way over to the stage. He handed me my diploma, smiled and then turned to the audience with his microphone.

"And we're especially proud of one of our top scholars this year, Lily Mitchell, who has received the coveted Parthin University Scholarship. She'll be studying at the University of Parthin this coming fall."

My face grew, if possible, even more red. Mom had no idea about the scholarship, and I hadn't planned to tell her. This ruined everything. I smiled stiffly and hurried off the stage as fast as I could.

The ceremony finally ended, and mom met me in the stands. "Congratulations, honey!" She hugged me tightly and smiled at me, tearing up all over again. "Why didn't you tell me you got a scholarship?"

"I...forgot," I replied lamely.

Before she could say anything, Crystal walked up and nudged me. "Hi, Mrs. Mitchell. I was wondering if Lily could come spend the night tonight."

She winked at me. I'd totally forgotten about the party. After the principals' embarrassing announcement, I was in no mood to go anywhere, but mom nodded, trapping me.

"Yeah, I think that should be fine. Have fun sweetie, and we'll talk about your scholarship later."

"But..."

She hurried off, pulling out her keys as she went. I knew what she'd say when I got home. She'd always wanted me to go to college since she never got the chance, but how could I? There was no way I'd go to school six hours away while she suffered. At the same time, though, I felt a sharp pang of jealousy and regret. I wanted to go to college more than anything. I'd planned on it my whole life. All of my classmates swirled around me, talking excitedly about plans after high school and telling everyone where they were going to college. I looked at my best friends angrily. We'd planned to live together in a dorm, decorate it ourselves, take all the same classes, but all that had changed now. Only they would get to go, leaving me behind in this smoggy, awful place.

"Lily?" Crystal looked at me expectantly. Cherie stood next to her, smiling and waving at someone else. I mustered up a smile and followed my friends, wishing more than anything I could just go home and crawl into bed.

Chapter Six

I shifted uncomfortably in my seat in Crystal's ancient rusty, red Camaro. We looked ridiculous. Cherie and Crystal got way too excited, put on a ton of makeup, miniskirts and tank tops, then forced me to do the same. How could I have fun when I had to yank my skirt down every five minutes?

"This is going to be the most awesome party," said Crystal. "I heard Brock Allen and some of his friends talking about it yesterday and they said there's supposed to be a pool and a strobe light and lasers and a DJ with like, every song ever written…"

I tuned Crystal out and stared at the road flashing by. All I could think about was mom. My insides still twisted with guilt every time I thought of her happy smile at the thought that I was spending time with friends on Friday night. She wouldn't smile if she knew where I really went.

We finally pulled through the Hanson house gates and parked on the lawn. The curb and driveway were already packed. Ted lived in a rich neighborhood called Overlook Cove, which sat on a road that ran right alongside the beach cliffs. People here were accustomed to five or six room mansions with tennis courts and pools and all the like. Teenagers already scattered all over the yard, some drinking out of paper cups, others jumping or swaying in groups to the loud music. We got out and were immediately assaulted by the nerds.

"Hey baby, what's shakin'?" said some drunken dork in coke-bottle-bottom glasses. I ignored him and pushed through the crowd towards the house.

"Your loss, baby!"

Cherie and Crystal giggled. "What a loser!" Cherie said, tossing her hair. We had to overstep people who'd passed out, toilet paper rolls, cups, bras and other weird things on our way to the front door. My feeling of discomfort only grew when we walked through the front door. Several people crowded around a guy chugging beer, while a couple girls slid down the banisters, laughing their heads off. I tugged on my skirt again, trying to make sure that at least a part of my legs were covered. Cherie and Crystal, on the other hand, seemed completely in their element.

Crystal drifted off with a couple boys who wanted to dance in the chandeliered living room, while Cherie ducked into the kitchen after Walt Jamison, her latest crush. I stood uncomfortably in the front hall before making my way to the wall. I'd never been good with parties and never would be. I felt frozen in a huge spotlight, even though no one looked at me.

I finally edged into the living room and sat down on a couch that wasn't already occupied by a couple making out. I felt so dumb for being here and for looking the way I did. Crystal and Cherie wouldn't want to leave for at least another couple hours. I had absolutely nothing to do. I tried closing my eyes and imagining the surf with the perfect waves curling over my head to shut out all the noise when something suddenly brushed my bare arm.

"Did I wake you up?"

I opened my eyes and looked over into Wes's teasing face. I wanted to say something sarcastic or snooty, but I couldn't come up with anything.

"No," I replied sullenly. "Parties aren't really my thing."

I felt like I had just told him that I still slept with my old stuffed penguin at night. He stared into my eyes like he usually did. I looked away, unable to look at him.

"Are you here by yourself?"

"No, my friends came. We rode in Crystal's car." Why did I say that? He didn't know who Crystal was. And why did I feel so dumb around him all the time?

"It *is* kind of a crazy party," he said quietly. "Turns out, Ted's older brother heard about it, and since there weren't any good parties up at the university, he decided to bring his college buddies down. They're really trashing the place."

As he said it, a sound came from the fancy parlor like a chair crashing on a grand piano.

"Ouch," he said, wincing. "I'd hate to be Ted right now."

I laughed. "I've never understood that," I replied. "I mean, why people think it's ok to come over to a complete stranger's house and destroy the place."

"Yeah, those rotten kids," he laughed, shaking his fist like an angry neighbor.

"That's not what I meant!"

But Wes kept laughing and I couldn't help laughing along with him. He sounded just like a ninety year-old man with rowdy neighbors.

"Do you want to leave? It sounds like your friends can take care of themselves." Goosebumps suddenly erupted all over my arms. I put my hands behind my back to hide them.

"I…well…have you been…you know, drinking?" I cringed as I said it. I'd be eighteen in a little over a month, but I acted like a scared thirteen year-old.

"No. Scout's honor, I swear." He winked at me. "You can trust me, I wouldn't lie. Drinking isn't really my thing."

I looked into his deep, greenish hazel eyes, feeling strangely like I could trust him completely. I even forgot to be sarcastic in my desperation to get out of the party as soon as possible.

"Let me just tell my friends," I said. "Wait for me here."

I took off like a shot so he wouldn't see my reddening face. The crowd became impossible to navigate. In the ten minutes I'd been at the party, the group of people doubled. I pushed and elbowed my way through until I finally got to the kitchen. Cherie still leaned against the counter, tossing her long, cinnamon-colored hair back over her shoulder as she laughed at Walt's joke. She looked around curiously when I said her name.

"I'm getting a ride home with…a friend," I muttered quickly.

"Who?" she asked, her voice tinged with excitement.

"None of your beeswax. I'll see you and Crystal later."

"It's Wes, isn't it?" she said, momentarily forgetting about Walt. I didn't answer, just ducked back into the crowd before she could get too excited. I finally made my way back to Wes, carefully stepping over a guy who's just started puking in someone's backpack.

When Wes saw me, he took my hand without another word and led me through the front door. The same people, some slumped in oblivion and others drinking, were still scattered across the lawn. We picked our way carefully through the mess. Wes got to the party early enough to park on the driveway. He unlocked the passenger door to his sleek white car and let me inside, gently closing the door after me. It was an older car, but with nicer features than mine. The air conditioning actually worked, something I'd never enjoyed in my own car.

After about a million hairpin turns on both driveway and grass, Wes finally managed to maneuver out of the yard and through the gate to the road.

"You really don't like parties, do you?" he asked, glancing casually over at me before turning his eyes back to the road. He must have heard my sigh of relief as we drove away.

"It's not that I'm like, a hermit or something," I muttered. "I just get uncomfortable…"

I trailed off, feeling dumber than ever, but Wes didn't seem to notice. He winked good-naturedly at me.

"I know what you mean. Ted's a good friend, that's really the only reason I showed up. Kinda glad to leave, actually."

"Oh…good." Wow. How could he not faint over my witty articulation? I drifted awkwardly into silence, not really knowing what else to say. Luckily, Wes picked up the slack.

"Where do you live?" he asked.

I tensed my shoulders nervously. Wes lived close to the beach, so he lived in a decent neighborhood. I paused, not wanting to tell him, but I didn't really have a choice. I could tell him somewhere else, but walking home at this hour is just asking for trouble.

"Cherry Lane."

"Um…yeah, near Front Street, right?"

I could hear the implication in his voice. Front Street, the most dangerous street in the city. And I lived two blocks away from it. I nodded, not even able to bring myself to look at him.

"Address?"

"713," I whispered. He drummed his fingers on the steering wheel, clearly uneasy and out of things to say.

"I couldn't help but notice what a good surfer you are," he said suddenly, sounding glad to have something else to talk about. "You were hitting that wave perfect before you fell."

"Um, thanks."

"Have you been surfing long?"

I twiddled my fingers a little, debating how to answer. I'm a good surfer. *Really* good. And I've been surfing since I could practically swim, but I didn't want to sound full of it.

"Um…a while," I replied lamely.

He smiled. "You know, my buddies and I were going to go down to the beach on Sunday. There's supposed to be a perfect swell around eight or so. You and your friends can come, if you want."

"Are you asking me on a date again?" I looked at him sharply.

"Hey, you said it, not me," he answered with the same swaggerish as when we'd talked in Study Hall. "But, I mean, I did say you could bring your friends and all, so it doesn't have to be a date. I know how you hate the mention of the 'D' word."

I looked at his face, considering. He'd become a complete mystery to me. Before, it was easy to write him off as another popular jock who got gold stars in every subject. Senior class treasurer, class clown, pretty cute, decent surfer…but the more we talked, the more I found different layers, deeper emotions and thoughts. It bothered and intrigued me. Is he interested in me? Or is he just being nice? Why would I even wonder?

I tried hard to push it from my mind, but the lingering doubts kept surfacing. It couldn't hurt to go surfing with him, since Cherie and Crystal would be with me. Maybe he really did just want to be friends, after all.

"Yeah…I mean, I guess that would be alright," I finally replied.

Wes didn't say anything back since we pulled onto Front Street. He drove as fast as he could through the crowds of druggies and bums wandering down both sidewalks and across the street. Then we flew around a corner and up onto Cherry Lane.

"You live in the big complex?" he asked.

I nodded as he glanced over. He was visibly afraid now, but was trying not to show it. My cheeks burned as we pulled into my parking garage.

He jumped out and circled the car to my side, glancing around nervously as he did. I stepped out when he opened my door.

"I'll walk you up," he offered as he shut the door.

"You don't have to." Even though I knew I lived in one of the worst neighborhoods in the city, I still thought he could be a little less obvious about being terrified to walk me to my door.

"I'm not letting you walk alone," he said. "Especially at night."

"I do it all the time." I couldn't help rolling my eyes. Technically, I didn't really walk alone at night. Only a few times. Mom maintained a strict curfew, which I broke a few times.

"I don't care," he said, taking my hand. Even through my indignation, I felt that now-familiar sweeping sense of euphoria from his touch. We walked up the stairs to my door, his hand cupped firmly around mine.

He paused before the door and looked me in the eyes. "Did I just imagine it, or did you say you might want to go surfing with me?"

"Well…I, I mean…my friends and I, yeah." Well, if Wes previously had any interest in me, it probably disappeared right then.

"Sweet," he replied. "Meet us at the beach at seven-thirty then."

"Ok."

He took both my hands again in his and stared down at me. "Listen, I'm sorry."

"For what?"

"I…I didn't mean to act like a jerk back there, being uncomfortable here and all. It's not that I…"

"It's fine," I cut him off. "I know it's not the best. We couldn't help it. My dad picked up and left and my mom and I don't have much. It's all we can afford."

I stopped talking abruptly, mortified. He'd probably tell me to just forget Sunday, but he surprised me by resting his hands gently on my arms.

"It's ok, Lily, I understand. And it doesn't change the fact that I want to get to know you better."

I tried to say something back, but the words caught in my throat. I'd never met a guy who so genuinely cared. My respect for him rose a couple notches. Actually, quite a few notches.

"I'll see you on Sunday," he whispered with a smile. He walked past me, down the stairs into the parking garage, leaving me breathless and extremely confused.

Chapter Seven

Sunday morning dawned bright and a little chilly for June. My back ached, my eyes stung from having spent the night listening for my mom to call. She hadn't, but the worry persisted every day and into the night.

I groaned slightly as I shifted in my blankets and sat up. Only surfing could pull me out of bed at this ungodly hour after virtually no sleep.

Ten minutes later, I stood in the bathroom in my bikini, gathering my hair up in a messy bun. Crystal and Cherie would mock me for wearing my red one today, thinking that I'd worn it to impress Wes. They'd practically cackled when I told them about the surfing invite. I usually didn't wear my red bikini, but all the others desperately needed washing. Mom always jokes that I have more bathing suits than normal clothes, but when you're in the water all the time, they're kind of a necessity.

I hurried through the living room, trying to move fast before mom woke from her perch in the chair.

"Hold it."

"Crap," I said under my breath. I turned around to face mom, my hands clutched around my surfboard.

"Yeah?" I said casually.

"Are you going surfing?"

"Yes…"

"You know how I feel about that, Lily." She sighed impatiently. "I don't want you in the water after your accident."

"Mom, I'll be fine! I've been out thousands of times and I've only had a few accidents."

"Honey, I just don't want you…"

"I know, I know, you don't want me getting eaten by sharks or drowned," I finished for her.

"It's not just that, Lily, it's…" She trailed off, peaking my curiosity instantly.

"What?"

"Nothing." She set her lips in a firm line.

"Mom, what?"

"It doesn't matter." She stared up at me with dull, tired eyes.

"Look, it's just for an hour or so, and I'll be with lots of other people." I arranged my face into my best pleading gesture. Normally, I would have opted to stay with mom. Part of me wondered why I wanted to go, but I pushed away the thought immediately.

"Like that boy who dropped you off the other night?"

I felt my mouth drop in surprise. How on earth had she found out about that?

"Lily, I'm your mom. I may be old, but I'm not dumb."

"But how…"

She grinned sheepishly. "I heard you coming up the stairs and took a peek out of the window. But what I *don't* understand is why you planned to spend the night at Crystals' house and wound up coming home early with some boy."

I suddenly became very interested in my feet. "We went to a party," I mumbled to my pink sparkly toes. "I didn't want to stay, so Wes brought me home."

I could hear her angry huff and imagined the stern look on her face. "You know how I feel about parties, Lily. I was considering letting you go surfing, but maybe I shouldn't."

"Mom, please! I'm sorry, I should have told you, but I swear I didn't drink or anything. Crystal and Cherie talked me into it, I didn't want to go, I swear!" I looked up at her and did my best Bambi-eyes impression.

"I'm glad you didn't drink, but it's not that," she replied in a measured voice. "It's the fact that you lied to me about where you were going."

"I'm sorry, mom. I promise it won't happen again."

I finally raised my head to look at her. I figured she'd look angry, annoyed at best, but the look on her face shocked me. Terror filled her eyes. She stared at me like she would lose me any minute. In the silence, I heard the local reporter encouraging people to come forward with any information about some random government people who went missing.

"All right," she finally replied. "Even though I shouldn't, I'll let you go since you already made plans. However, when you get home, no TV, no communicator. You can stay in your room for the day and work on your correspondence papers."

"Fair enough," I mumbled. We'd already argued about correspondence classes. Mom thought it would be good for me to do classes by communicator since I refused to leave for Parthin, but it didn't make my worry disappear. What if the administration made me go up there to take a test or something? I couldn't risk staying away from mom for more than a few hours at a time.

There's nothing I can do about it right now. I repeated this phrase to myself every so often. After mom's diagnosis, she made me see a psychologist to help me learn how to cope. He'd suggested that I repeat this phrase over and over instead of freaking out over what I couldn't control. After a while, I felt calm. I'd figure out the correspondence when I came home. I started towards the door when mom called me back.

"Lily...stay away from the woods."

I laughed in surprise. "The woods? What, are you talking about those old stories you used to tell me? About the scary beasts?"

"Lily, I just...there's been some really weird things happening on the news lately. I worry about you being out in general, let alone at the beach. The Mai..."

She stopped talking abruptly and fiddled with the remote control.

"What?" I asked, but she shook her head firmly. I glanced from the TV screen to mom. She'd been so glued to the news lately. She never really watched it before, but now she kept it on practically all day. Part of me wondered why, and what secrets she kept, but the clock read seven-fifteen. I couldn't worry about it now. I'd have time to ask her later.

"Mom, you know I can look after myself, and I never go into the woods. But thanks for the worry." I smiled and reached over to squeeze her hand reassuringly. "I'll be back by lunch."

"I love you, Lily." The tone of her voice raised a lump in my throat. The lines on her face made it clear that the pain kept getting worse. I swallowed hard, considering whether I should stay. But I turned towards the door.

"Love you too, mom. See you in a bit."

I stepped out into the morning, trying to forget the look on mom's face. The bums weren't milling around yet. It took some maneuvering to get down the small staircase with my board, but I finally made it down to the garage and to my trusty old truck, Sheila. Yes, I named my car, but I put up with the Clancy twins for two years straight to pay for her, so I figured she should have a name.

I tossed my board into the bed and climbed in. The engine roared to life, shattering the relative silence in the garage. As I pulled out, I noticed a skeletally thin man with almost-translucent skin sitting in the parking booth, even though the complex hadn't employed a parking attendant for years. He tipped his hat in greeting as I drove past, but far from friendly, his gesture seemed cold and threatening. An unexpected wave of fear passed over me as I pulled out and drove away. It was completely stupid, but somehow I knew that he watched me as I drove out of the parking garage and drove down Cherry to Front Street. I don't know why, but the parking attendant strongly reminded me of our creepy substitute in math class. I could almost imagine the same look of cold loathing on the attendants' face.

Chapter Eight

No way. It couldn't be. Mom just made me paranoid. I shrugged off the feeling and rolled down my window to let in the morning air. The pressing weight of depression of the city gradually lifted as I reached the highway. The thought of huge swells and cruising massive waves lifted my spirits.

Everyone was gathered on the beach by the time I pulled up and grabbed my board out of the back. Crystal and Cherie grinned slyly as they, and Wes, took in my red bikini. I should have worn a dirty one.

"How's the swell?" I said a little too loudly, trying to distract everyone.

Wes blinked a couple times and glanced out at the waves. "Um…they're ok right now, but it's supposed to get better by around eight." For the first time, he stared at me like every other guy did, his eyes taking me in. I wanted badly to reach for the T-shirt in my bag and cover up.

"So what are we doing until then?" I said, sounding bossy even to myself.

"Well…we could go for a swim," said Wes.

"Yeah, definitely," said a tall, blonde guy I didn't recognize. He grabbed Crystal's hand and pulled her towards the shore while she giggled hysterically. The other guy, Walt Jamison, grabbed Cherie's hand and started to pull her towards the water too. He liked her as much as she liked him, apparently.

"Wait, wait, I haven't put on sunscreen yet!" she shrieked, but Walt picked her up, cradling her, and ran towards the water. I narrowed my eyes at Wes. He shrugged with an embarrassed grin.

"Hey, I didn't know they were all going to take off."

"Whatever," I muttered. Clutching my board, I marched off towards the shore. The cold water felt like an electric shock, but I plunged in anyway. I'd get used to it soon.

"Is it so terrible to be alone with me?" said Wes somewhere behind me. "You shouldn't surf alone, you know! *Especially after what happened last time!*" He had waded into the water and placed his board gently on the water. I hopped onto my board and started paddling out, completely ignoring him. He followed me at a safe distance, which only irritated me more.

The farther I paddled, the waves became more intense. A large wave rose in the distance. I paddled out furiously to try and catch it before it crested. I managed to ride up the side of the wave just as the foam appeared, but something shot past me before I could get to my feet. Wes came up from behind me and coasted down the wave.

Under my wave of anger, I felt a surge of admiration. He surfed perfectly, moving his board gracefully across the water. I popped up on my board and flew down the wave after him, trying to show him up. He looked back at me and grinned. He'd duped me into playing his little game, showing me up just for attention. Jerk.

I pointed my board down the wave and let it propel me to the shore. A small cove sat in the distance, so I knelt down on my board and paddled hard towards it. One last small wave finally pushed me into the cove, where I climbed up on the rocky ledges. I dragged my board up with me and looked out at the entrance. Wes followed me in, a wide grin on his face.

"Seriously, can I just have a minute *alone*?" I shouted, not realizing how angry I'd gotten.

"Man, when you play hard to get, you really play hard to get!"

"Well, you're not getting anywhere with me, so you can just turn around and paddle your huge, expensive board out of here!"

His face fell. A quick, hot surge of guilt swept through me. He looked genuinely hurt. With a frown, he dragged his board up onto the rocks some distance away from me.

"What did I do wrong? Is it something I said?" He spoke just loudly enough to be heard over the crashing waves.

"Wes…no, but I just…"

"My board really isn't that expensive, you know," he muttered. "I got it at a yard sale in Overlook Cove couple years back. And yeah, you grew up in the slums, but life hasn't exactly been a picnic for me either. I have a dad, but half the time he's too drunk to function. My mom works herself to death to support us while he lazes around. I don't see her much."

His board floated in the water, attached to him by the ankle leash. The expensive brand label flaked in places.

"I'm…I'm sorry, Wes," I said.

Hot tears suddenly started flowing down my cheeks. They came without warning. I tried to hold them down, hide them, but not before he noticed. He splashed through the shallow water to the rocks where I sat. I felt his arm wrap around my bare shoulders.

"What's eating you, Lily?" he whispered in my ear. I wiped my streaming eyes and looked up at him.

"I don't have time for dating because my mom is dying," I choked. "She has cancer. One of the worst kinds."

The sobs took over again. Wes simply held me close and stroked my hair while I cried. After a while, I finally stopped crying and sniffled.

"I wish I knew what to say." He wiped a tear away. "I promise I wasn't trying to push you or anything. I just wanted to get to know you."

"It's ok." Surprisingly, my shoulders relaxed. Some of my constant tension slowly drained away. "It's not your fault."

"I know, but I can't imagine life without my mom. She's always been there for me, even with working odd hours."

I just shrugged, worried that the tears might start again. He gently touched my knee, sending more shivers up my spine.

"Lily, I know we just met and everything, but I want you to know that I'm here if you need anyone to talk to," he said hurriedly. He winced slightly, probably waiting for my attack. Instead, I smiled a weak, watery smile.

"Thanks, Wes. I'm sorry I didn't cut you more of a break before. I…I really appreciate your offer and everything."

A loud crash sounded outside the cove. We looked towards the opening and saw white foam swirling in every direction.

"Well, I don't know about you, but I'm not letting this perfect swell go to waste." He jumped onto his board and started paddling like a madman to get back out to sea. I strapped my ankle leash in place and dove into the water with my board, paddling furiously to keep up with him.

We hit tons of flawless waves, the best swells I'd seen in years. Wes glided in and out of the waves naturally, as if he'd done this all his life. Which he probably had.

"It feels like it's going down a bit," he said after a particularly big wave. He shook water out of his hair. "You wanna try tandem for a while? It's easier on smaller waves."

I'd never ridden on a board with anyone, and I honestly didn't feel comfortable trying it just yet, but I couldn't look like a weenie in front of him.

"Sure," I said, trying to sound confident. I headed towards shore and squinted against the sun to see where our friends went. They surfed down the beach, at least a quarter of a mile away. We drifted farther than I thought.

I climbed out of the water and crawled up the shore with Wes close behind. He chivalrously took my board and placed it safely far enough away from the water so the tide wouldn't reach it. He hoisted his longboard under his armpit and led me out to the water. He'd used a short board at the party. Maybe he's brought his long board on purpose…

I shook my head, not even wanting to think it. He isn't interested in me, I'm not interested in him. We're friends. That's it.

When we got deep enough to paddle, Wes helped me up on the board and then climbed up after me.

"Have you ever gone tandem before?" he asked.

"Um…no," I replied.

"Well, it's easy enough. You just pop up like you normally would, but then you have to scoot in front of me. We'll have to move-"

He stopped talking. A smaller wave crept towards us. Both of us paddled furiously. I popped up quickly and moved in front of Wes. He pulled me close to him, and for a few alarming seconds we wobbled on the board, close to falling over, but he shifted his weight and the board straightened out. We were balanced, but he didn't take his hands off my waist.

We wove gracefully through the water, both of us using our combined weight to navigate the crest and the small barrel. I'd thought tandem would be horrible, but we worked together well. What I had thought would be awkward and painful was actually really *incredible*.

After a while, the waves died down into baby waves until we couldn't surf anymore. He dove from the board into the water and splashed me playfully. I got ready to splash back when something on the cliffs above us distracted me. A man walked along the cliffs, watching us. He wore black pants and a black cloak, even though it had to be at least ninety degrees outside. Very dark sunglasses shielded his eyes from the morning sun. An uneasy shiver tingled slowly down my spine. He reminded me of someone…but who? Then it hit me. Even though he stood high above us, I felt the same eerie sense of doom that I'd felt around the creepy sub and the garage attendant.

I shrugged, trying to get rid of the dark feeling. Who was I kidding? Why would he want to watch us? Maybe mom's warning made it seem like everyone watched me.

"Um, we should probably find the others," I said distractedly. "I need to get home."

Wes looked slightly disappointed, but he covered it with a smile so quickly I almost thought I'd imagined it.

He climbed on the board in front of me and we paddled to the shore. Crystal, Cherie and their guys whispered and giggled when we walked over to them. I ignored them and glanced behind me. The man on the cliffs left, but the back of my neck still prickled with uneasiness. I tried to shrug it off again as I gathered my things.

I picked up my shorts and felt my communicator buzzing in the pocket. Several missed calls lit the screen.

"Angie," I spoke into the communicator quietly. She'd called about seven or eight times, something she didn't usually do. Angie's our neighbor and she hardly ever calls me. We normally talked on the communal balcony at the complex. The screen went black for a moment, then lit up as Angie's kindly face appeared, lined with worry and fatigue.

"Angie? What's going on?" I asked, my heart already plummeting to my feet at the look on her face.

"It's…your mom, honey. You need to get home quick."

Chapter Nine

Tears blurred my eyes, the emotion making my throat burn. The news I'd been dreading to hear since mom got diagnosed. *Is she dying for real? How could I have been so stupid and selfish, going surfing?*

I reached my car and fumbled with the lock and key. Finally, I wrenched the door open and tumbled into the seat, but something stopped the car door from shutting. I looked up frantically and saw Wes standing above me, a look of deep concern on his face.

"What's going on?"

"My mom…I have to go…"

"Let me drive you," he said.

"No! Get off my door, didn't you hear me? My mom!" The rational part of my brain registered that I totally sounded insane, but I didn't care.

"If you drive, you'll wreck! Let me help you for once!" he yelled.

I could feel precious minutes ticking by. I'd never be able to get rid of him.

"Fine! Just hurry up!"

I vaulted into the passenger side and let Wes slide into the driver's seat. He took just a moment to familiarize himself with the controls on my car before he shifted into drive and swung around towards the city.

Adrenaline made me hyper-alert and sensitive. I pushed the floor uselessly with my foot. Taking the hint, Wes pushed the accelerator and shot towards the city. We reached the city limits at Mach speed, and Wes wove his way skillfully through morning traffic. I didn't wait until he stopped the car in the complex garage to jump out and hurry up the stairs. My heart felt like a brick in my chest.

I got to the door just in time to see a hospital stretcher being angled out onto the small stairway. Mom lay strapped to the gurney, her eyes closed, her face a ghostly shade of gray.

I didn't care who I pushed or shoved to get to her. *I have to get to her before they do, before they took her away.*

"Mom," I gasped, reaching her side. I took her cold hand in mine.

"Honey," she said weakly. "I'm so sorry, honey…"

I felt a rush of relief knowing she was still alive, but she looked terrible.

"What happened?"

I figured maybe some of her vitals had dropped or maybe her medicine had stopped working, but it had happened before and a simple doctor's visit cured her. Why did she have to go to the hospital?

"That man…" She gave a low groan, her eyes shut tight.

"What?" Bewilderment somehow crept through my terror and panic. "What man?"

As far as I knew, there had never been a man in mom's life. Dad left before mom had me.

Suddenly, I felt pain in my wrist. One of the paramedics gripped it tightly, his eyes stern but kind.

"We need to move, miss. She needs to get to the hospital. Come to the ambulance with us." His voice didn't shake, just stayed firm and authoritative. He'd clearly dealt with hysterical relatives before.

Dimly, I thought of Wes, that he'd have no way home, but I couldn't worry about him now. Mom mattered most.

I followed the ambulance crew numbly as they rushed down the stairs and pushed the gurney through the double doors of the vehicle. I climbed in after mom. I thought we'd shoot off immediately, but someone argued near the doors, keeping us from going.

"Move!"

I turned to see Wes clambering in, shutting the doors behind him. He smiled tensely, but didn't say anything. I didn't bother asking how he'd convinced them to let him in. The driver shot forward with a bone-rattling jolt, the sirens screaming overhead. I wouldn't be able to hear him over the noise anyway.

I held onto mom's hand as we wove through the city streets to the hospital. I felt Wes's eyes on me, but I couldn't look back at him. I knew as much as he did that we'd connected on a deep level this morning, but how could I think of him at a time like this? My life felt complicated enough without feelings for him mixed in.

A few harried minutes later, we screeched to a halt in front of the hospital and left the ambulance. The workers tried to push mom away without me and I followed, frantic to keep up.

One man, the one who grabbed my wrist, held me back as mom went through double doors to a restricted area.

"You can't go in there, ma'am." He sounded tired now, not as authoritative as he did at my apartment. "She needs some tests, but you can wait until they're done and come see her."

I nodded mutely and stumbled over to the hard plastic chair in the waiting room. A warm hand touched my shoulder. Wes sat on the chair beside me, a look of deep sympathy on his face.

"I'm sorry, I didn't even think about how you would get home," I mumbled. He shrugged.

"It's ok, I'll just catch a cab." He tried to look casual with a good-natured smile, but it didn't quite hide his worry. "I don't live too far from here, so the fare won't even be that bad."

We sat silently for a while. I wanted to say something, tell him how thankful I was that he was here, that I wasn't facing this alone, but the words wouldn't come. Instead, I leaned my head on his shoulder. I could feel his surprise, but he responded quickly, leaning closer and wrapping his arm around me. It felt so good that I wanted to let down my walls for good. I wanted to let him in.

Hesitantly, I relaxed and allowed myself to really think about Wes, how I felt about him. I didn't hate him, even though I'd done my best to make him think that. We're friends, but I knew all along I felt more for him. A strange longing rose within me, a longing to hold him close, to wrap my arms around his strong shoulders and feel his lips pressed against mine, his fingers running through my hair and stroking my cheek...

I shook my head slightly. Why would I think about Wes that way at a time like this? It's ridiculous, like laughing at a funeral. And yet, the confusion kept swirling in my mind, threatening to overwhelm me like a towering swell in the ocean.

"Lily?" I looked up to see Dr. Dennison, our family doctor, standing above me. "You can see her, but I need to talk with you first."

I stood up, feeling achy all over. I followed him to the hospital desk and he turned towards me. The look on his face turned my stomach to ice.

"I've gotten your mom's vitals back up to par," he said quietly. "Seems she just had a bad shock. But…she's in really bad shape. The cancer has gotten worse since her last follow-up. She *needs* the Barbach treatment."

The doctors talked about the treatment before. I'd learned about it in school. Pierre Barbach, some scientist, discovered a cure for cancer in his research. Several of his patients were cured completely with no reoccurrence of tumors.

"Yeah, I've heard of it, Doc, but there's no way I'd be able to save up what it costs. Probably about a million, right?"

He hesitated. "About six thousand dollars, not including travel expenses to and from Ithaca. Unfortunately, that's the only place in the country that can offer the treatment right now."

"Great." I tried hard to keep the tears from coming, but they came, burning my throat and constricting my voice. "We don't have that. My mom can't work, and we're barely surviving on compensation from the Mainframe."

"Can you work?" he asked.

"I'm still a kid!" I knew I sounded hysterical, but I didn't care. "I'm not even eighteen yet!"

"You're old enough to work at least part time. You've already graduated high school, haven't you?" I heard an edge in his voice. How could he talk to me like that? What other eighteen year old has to deal with stuff like this?

"I have a part-time job for the summer, but I can't work full-time. I have to take care of mom." It was a bit of a white lie, but I thought about running a tutoring business for summer-schoolers.

"Well…it looks like you have some choices to make. The Mainframe will only support you until you turn eighteen, then you're on your own. They'll continue to support your mother since she's disabled, but you need a job. And the sooner the better, because I don't think she has more than three months at the most."

"How is that supposed to be enough time to save up money and get her a treatment?"

"The time is just a guesstimate, she may have longer." He looked at me over the rim of his glasses. "Why can't you work full time now that you're out of school? You're not going back in the fall, and I presume you're not going to University."

"Like I told you, I have to take care of mom. We don't have any family around. Besides, it's not like I'd be earning adult wages."

"Well, Lily, in my experience, I've found that when you do everything you can, things work out."

"Gee, thanks, I'll log that away." I knew he was trying to help, but saying meaningless words wouldn't cure her cancer. "Can I see my mom now?"

"Yes."

He started walking down the hall to her room when I remembered Wes. I turned around to see what had happened to him. He stood by his chair with his communicator in hand.

"I better head out," he said. "I figured you would want some time alone."

He turned to leave, but I grabbed his hand and pulled him back. "Wes...thank you. For everything."

He touched my chin gently and lifted my face to his. "You're welcome. Hang in there. Things will look up." He suddenly wrapped me in his arms and held me close, sending a cascade of chills all over my body. An odd mixture of emotions flowed through me; pain, fear, confusion and that same strange longing. I wanted to push him away, but I didn't want to let him go. I wanted him with me when I saw my mom, but I knew I couldn't ask him to stay. I needed to be with mom right now.

With one last squeeze of my hand, he pulled away and left, walking down the hall towards the double doors that led to the main lobby. Waves of emotion crashed over me as I stood there, not quite knowing what to think.

I turned and walked slowly down the hall to mom's room. She sat propped up on the pillows, her face pale, dark purple shadows under her closed eyes.

I sat quietly, thinking she'd been put to sleep, but she opened her eyes.

"Oh, good, it's you," she said with a weak smile. "I thought it was another nurse coming to poke me again."

I tried to smile, but could only manage a grimace. "Mom, are you ok?"

"Oh, honey...I'm all right." She wore her strong expression, the one she saved for when I occasionally broke down from the weight of it all. "This is so unfair for you. You should be out with your friends, enjoying your summer instead of here with me. You've had to grow up so fast lately."

I started crying again. Mom held out her arms to me. I squeezed into the small space on the bed next to her and let her wrap her arms around me. She held me for a while, stroking my hair like she used to when I was a little girl.

"I want to be with you, mom," I sobbed. "I don't want to be anywhere else."

"I'm sorry, Lily," she said again, her voice a little off. The nurse must have given her a sedative for the pain. She sounded like she struggled to stay awake.

"Why are you sorry?" I whispered back.

"I just wish you weren't growing up in all this," she replied. "I wish you had a normal life."

"It's not your fault you got sick." I looked up at her face with its sunken cheeks and pale, sallow skin. She looked more frail than I'd ever seen her. A sudden, fierce wave of determination swept through me. I'd work until I dropped if I had to. She'd get that surgery, no matter what I had to do.

"I know, Lily, but I just wish I could give you more. I wish I had more time."

A single tear crept from her eye, down her cheek and dropped gently onto her neck.

"Mom, you're not going to die. I won't let it happen." My voice cracked like brittle ice.

"Lily…the doctors…"

"The doctors say a lot of things. I won't let it happen."

"No, Lily, I mean…more time to explain…"

"Explain what?"

"Strange things…"

The drugs won over. Her eyelids, heavy with induced sleep, couldn't hold themselves up any longer.

"Mom? What strange things?"

I guessed I'd talked a little too loud because a nurse came hurrying in and checked the I.V.

"Look, honey, I know you want to stay with your mom, but maybe it's better that you leave. Go home and get some rest. For crying out loud, you're in nothing but a bathing suit and T-shirt."

She frowned, as if I'd planned to show up scantily clad just to cause a scene. Honestly, I'd just forgotten. Surfing with Wes seemed like a million years ago now instead of just this morning.

"But she was saying something about strange things-"

"She's on some pretty intense painkillers," the nurse replied. "She probably thinks the sky is purple too."

"Then why are you putting her on the crap?" I snapped. Mom's hand tightened around mine. I looked down to see her finally slip into unconsciousness. Her grip loosened until her hand fell loosely on the bed.

"It's helping her sleep so the pain won't make her scream." I could tell the nurse wanted me gone, that she didn't want some teenager in a swimsuit ruining her routine checks, but she'd just have to deal with it.

"Well, I'll stay here with her if you don't mind. I'm not a baby, I think I can handle myself."

"Fine." She gestured to the only armchair in the room, a cushy chair with ugly pink plastic upholstery. "At least sit down."

I plopped down in an angry huff and waited for her to leave. After typing a few more things into her dataclip, she finally walked out the door and down the hall, her rubbery shoes squeaking on the tile.

Left with nothing to do, I picked up the remote and started flipping through channels. None of my favorite shows popped up, so I clicked over to the news. I hardly ever watched the news, but I really didn't want to just sit there and listen to mom's shallow breathing.

"And now we'll hear from Victor Channing, head of the Department of Defense," said the black-uniformed reporter on TV. The camera switched over to a greasy-looking man sitting at a desk. He wore fancy clothes, but it looked like he cared more about his clothes than personal grooming. His hair held enough grease to start a fire.

"Thanks, Nancy," he said, his voice as oily as his hair. "As the citizens of Illyria are aware, the Southern Province of Epirus has created nothing but problems for our economy. The pollution seeping up from their nuclear waste plants has destroyed our soil. They have taken our livelihood and crushed it with their mindless expansion to the point where we have resorted to living off of rations. It is time we take back what was rightly ours, for the greater good. The great nation of Illyria will rise once again."

His comment triggered something in my memory, something that I learned in school a long time ago. One of my teachers, Mr. Allen, said something about pollution my sophomore year. He explained that our soil became toxic because of something that had happened a long time ago. Something here in Arduba, the capitol city of Illyria, not Epirus.

Mr. Allen told us something completely different from what this disgusting guy on TV said. An uneasy feeling crept into the pit of my stomach. Maybe mom *did* know something, something she tried to tell me just now before the drugs kicked in. This man, and what mom said, were connected somehow. I didn't know how, but they were.

Chapter Ten

I came home Monday evening after spending Sunday night in the hospital. Mom begged me to go sleep in a real bed and change into some warm clothes. She also reminded me that Crystal and Cherie planned to leave for Parthin the next day, so I needed to go say goodbye.

But I didn't want to. They'd been my best friends for practically forever, but seeing them only reminded me of everything I'd miss out on. They'd get to live the life that I secretly wished I could. I loved mom, and I couldn't leave her, but the tiniest part of me felt awful. I wished I could be like them, a normal teenager with nothing to worry about but exams and tuition.

As I stepped inside, I noticed that the apartment seemed too quiet. Mom usually had the TV on, but the built-in wall screen stayed black and silent. I wandered aimlessly into the kitchen and poured myself a bowl of cereal, but only ate about half of it before dumping it in the sink.

Mom and I didn't get to talk about anything since she'd slept most of the time. When she woke up, she only talked about using my scholarship for correspondence classes. Even though I brought up her weird remarks several times, she purposely avoided it. She claimed that the drugs made her say funny things, but I couldn't shake the doubt I felt about the whole thing. She *knew* something, but for some reason she didn't want to tell me. I especially wondered about the man she mentioned.

I also thought non-stop about the guy from the Defense Department. I tried and tried but couldn't remember what Mr. Allen told us two years ago. Something about the whole thing made me feel weird. I could almost imagine being one of the people in the stories I used to read about the old world wars, stories of people sitting in basements waiting for bombs to fall from airplanes above.

Finally, I couldn't take it anymore. Restlessness drove me crazy, so I decided to go down to the beach and take a walk. Fresh air would do me good. I felt completely exhausted from trying to sleep in that dumb pink chair, but I knew if I lay down I'd only go crazier. I locked all the bolts on the door securely and headed down to the parking garage.

"Evening, miss," said a voice behind me as I typed in the code to unlock my truck. The voice made me jump a mile and type in the wrong number.

I turned to see a tall, thin man with a weird smile standing behind me. He wore a black suit with red trim, the common uniform of the workers in the Mainframe. I could tell by the insignia on his lapels and his cap that he ranked highly. I peered closely at him and gasped. He'd been at my school, watching the line for the metal detectors. The one who'd stared at me.

I didn't bother answering. I concentrated on the key, trying not to look afraid. A visit from a Mainframe official is unusual at best. Two encounters with the same Mainframe official is about as bad as it can get.

"I spoke to your mother earlier. I heard she had a rather unfortunate spell in the hospital." His voice sent prickles of fear along my neck.

"So you're the jerk responsible for stressing her out," I grunted, trying to sound tough as I slowly typed in the numbers. I didn't want him to see my code and know how to break into my car. The code finally connected and the door clicked. "She has cancer, so I'd appreciate it if you'd stay away and quit scaring her."

"I'm so sorry if I caused you inconvenience." Yeah, right. He acted so sorry.

"Well, you should be. If you'll excuse me, I need to leave."

"Just one moment." He gently put a hand on my shoulder, but the effect terrified me instead of reassuring me. The moment he touched me, I felt like I'd been plunged into my worst nightmare. Every horrible memory I'd ever had flooded back through my mind at hyper speed, making me feel nauseous and weak. I jerked away and the feeling left as quickly as it had come.

"Get out of my way!" I hissed through clenched teeth.

"So sorry, miss, I tend to...startle people. I just wanted to talk to you about what I asked your mother. As you know, the Southern Province is a threat. We're looking to recruit good, young soldiers to our army."

"Not interested." I opened my door pointedly, hoping he'd

get the hint, but he didn't move.

"Oh, I'm sure you'll change your mind in time." He leaned closer and I noticed a slightly manic gleam in his eye. A tidal wave of fear swept through me. For the first time in my life, I wished I carried a weapon with me.

"Why would I want to sign up to go kill people? Get your Mainframe drones to do it."

The gleam in his eyes intensified. I knew without him telling me that I'd gone too far.

"Oh, don't worry, my young friend." His tone stayed as even and mellow, but a kind of vindictiveness crept into his eyes as he watched me. "Our soldiers won't fight. We're forming an army as more of a…message to the Southern Province, so that they don't get any ideas."

"I'm leaving now." I climbed in quickly and shut the door, my heart pounding in my ears. The creepy man didn't move. He stood rooted to the same spot, uncomfortably close to my car, as I reversed and sped out of the garage. I turned around, tires squealing, and saw him lift his hand to his hat and tip it slightly in my direction. I screeched out of the garage without checking for traffic. I almost preferred that he'd threatened me with a gun or something. I could handle that, but his weird calmness unnerved me. He acted too sure of himself, too sure of the fact that I'd join up someday. Not to mention the fact that I'd gone into some kind of vortex of blackness when he touched me. I'd never felt anything like it before. He isn't normal. How could he work for the Mainframe?

Evening traffic clogged the main bypass through the city. I clenched my hands around the wheel until the knuckles turned white. Every bum that passed my car, every car door closing or honk made me jump. I didn't breathe easily again until I turned onto the highway to the beach.

Chapter Eleven

An unusually cold coastal wind whipped across the cliffs as I picked my way down the cliff path. I'd only worn an old tank top and shorts, so I huddled down into the ridges in the rocks and wrapped my arms tightly around me. I should have just stayed home for all the good this did. I'd probably be blown away any minute.

"Hey," said a voice behind me. I scraped my knee on the rocks as I turned around. The creepy Mainframe dude in my parking garage had made me more than just a little jumpy. Wes stood behind me, wearing a light sweatshirt and faded jeans.

I breathed a sigh of relief. "What are you doing here?"

"I just…needed to get out for a while. I come up here sometimes just to watch the waves."

He looked uncomfortable as he rubbed the back of his neck with his hand. He sat down beside me and pulled off his sweatshirt. I took it gratefully and pulled it over my head.

"You look cold." His usual smile flickered over his obvious anxiety. What could make him look so afraid? He'd never been like this in the time I'd known him.

"Well, it is *supposed* to be summer." He smiled and scooted closer to me. I felt the same strange desire I'd felt in the hospital rising in me. I wanted to hold him, kiss him and take his fear and worry away. I carefully arranged my face into a nonchalant expression, hoping he couldn't read my thoughts in my eyes.

"How's your mom doing?" he asked.

"She's…alright, but the doctor says she needs the Barbach treatment."

He gave a low whistle. "That's pretty expensive, isn't it?"

I nodded. "I have no idea how I'm going to save up for it, but I have to."

Wes looked at me, his eyebrows raised. "You're looking for work?"

"Yeah."

"Well, I work over at the Ration Center and they need a replacement. It's not super glorious or anything, but it's a job. The pay is decent, too."

"Really?"

"Yeah. I'll let them know you're looking. They'll probably thank me since…"

"Since what?"

He pursed his lips and stared back out at the waves.

"What's wrong?"

He looked over at me and shrugged. "Nothing," he replied good-naturedly.

"You're lying. You've been worried since you got here. I can tell."

He turned to stare out at the waves again and took a deep breath. "I had to quit. I got a job in the Defense Department at the Mainframe. It's the only way to keep from getting recruited right now."

He wrapped his arms around his long, lanky legs and rested his chin on his knees. I fought the urge to put my arm around his shoulder.

"They're trying to recruit you?"

"Yeah. My mom's worried sick, so she pulled some strings with people she knows and got me a job as a developer. It's still no guarantee, but it'll buy me a little time."

"You make it sound like they've already shipped out troops," I said with a small laugh.

"They have," he said, before I'd even finished talking. His answer took me completely by surprise.

"*What*? How do you know?"

"I heard it on the Subversive."

"The Subversive?"

"It's on an unknown frequency on the communicators. They tell what's *really* going on about the war without the Mainframe knowing. The news makes it sound like we haven't even invaded yet, but we have."

I sat still, stunned into silence. I didn't really know what to say, so I just stared out at the pounding surf. The creepy man from the garage flashed into my mind and I shuddered a little.

"What?" he asked, noticing my reaction.

I looked over at him, considering. Part of me still felt a little guarded, like I couldn't completely let him in, but a bigger part of me was giving in to those hazel eyes and his little boy smile. He'd seen me at my absolute worst already, even though we'd only been talking to each other for a couple weeks.

"Something…weird happened." I decided I could trust him, since he trusted me.

He cocked his head. "What?"

I told him about the weird man in the garage. He scowled, and as I talked, his scowl grew deeper.

"Lily, that's not typical," he said darkly.

"What do you mean?" Flutters of panic rose in my chest. He looked angry and even a little afraid. Unsettled. Terror rose up in my heart like vile acid, eating away at my senses, letting panic invade. I'd never seen him like this before.

"The Mainframe Defense Personnel don't normally make personal visits. They've contacted me, but I received a summons to the Mainframe building like every other guy our age. That's where they explained the recruiting process and pretty much told me I had two months to sign up or they'd sign me up anyway. And besides, I've never heard of them contacting a girl. No offense."

"None taken." I sat for a moment, lost in my own thoughts. Why would the Mainframe have such an interest in me? It didn't make any sense at all. There was nothing special about me.

"Maybe they're just going around taking a survey, seeing who would be interested," he said. His tone made it clear that he was trying to convince himself more than trying to convince me.

"Maybe." I said it to make myself feel better, but I couldn't shake off the doubt. The encounter with the man did feel abnormal, completely out of the ordinary. He'd been so insistent that I would join up. I left out the part about him being the same man at school that day, since I felt terrified as it was.

Suddenly, I didn't want to talk or even think about it anymore. I felt a sudden, urgent need to talk to mom. She knew something that she wasn't telling me, but I'd get it out of her somehow.

"Anyway," said Wes, breaking into my thoughts, "I'm glad I found you here. We didn't get much time to talk after, well, you know."

I felt a huge surge of guilt. I'd been so horrible to Wes and he was sensitive enough to not mention my mom's stint in the hospital. I'd talked to and flirted with other boys before now, but it had all been shallow. Wes became different to me somehow, so much more profound. I'd never been so terrified of opening myself to anyone, but I slowly took his hand and laced my fingers through his. He smiled again, every trace of worry wiped from his face.

"I'm glad too," I whispered.

Wes glanced down at my hand in his. Suddenly, I felt too bold, too forward. *Does he think I'm cheap?* I started to take my hand away, but Wes clung to it, not wanting to let go.

"Lily…I have to tell you something," he said. "I stopped by your apartment to see you, but nobody answered, so I figured you might be here. I promise I'm not stalking you or anything, I just…I really wanted to see you."

He said it in a rush, looking a little worried. He'd come so far from the cocky, confident boy on the beach that day. Here with me on the cliffs, I realized that he probably felt more nervous than I did. My longing became more urgent, turning into a desperate need. I'd never felt so drawn to someone before. I grabbed his other hand and pulled him a little closer.

"It's ok," I replied. "I wanted to see you, too. I wanted to tell you how sorry I am."

"For what?" His voice grew husky. The sound of it made goose bumps rise all over my skin.

"For being so harsh. I like you, a lot. I just didn't want to get involved with anyone. No one knows how I feel, what I go through every day. I'm so worried about my mom that relationships just seemed pointless because she needs me-"

I started crying, feeling completely exposed. I'd never told anyone, even Cherie or Crystal, about how hard life had been since mom got sick. I looked up at Wes, expecting him to freak out from all the emotion. What I saw startled me. His eyes were soft and warm, full of feeling. I felt my heart race as he stood and pulled me up with him. He hugged me, putting his comforting arms tightly around me. I buried my face in his shoulder and pulled him closer, never wanting to let go of his comforting warmth.

Chapter Twelve

Wes and I stayed on the beach talking for a long time, making me tired the next day. I'd never met a guy like him. Most guys I'd dated before were into cars, or sports, or a mix of both. Wes liked all the typical guy things, but he also liked sophisticated things like history and art. He always considered me, asked how I felt, what I thought about things. He did so many things differently that unsettled me at first, then excited me.

I thought of him as I drove down Freemont Street towards Cherie's house to keep my spirits up. She and Crystal were meeting there and driving up to Parthin together. I hadn't gotten a chance to say goodbye the night before, so I'd see them before they took off.

I pulled up by the curb in front of Cherie's old ranch-style house. I loved Cherie's house. It'd been built several years ago as a retirement home for an old couple wanting to live near the coast. Years passed and a whole neighborhood had been built around it, but it still held some kind of old, mysterious charm.

She and Crystal already stood in the driveway, loading up their things, laughing as they shoved furniture into Cherie's tiny car. I felt my heart sink a little.

"Hey guys," I said as I climbed out of my truck.

"Lily! We were wondering when you going to come by." Crystal smiled warmly and I managed a weak smile back.

"I wouldn't miss saying goodbye. You guys are my best friends." I got a small bag out of my car and carried it over. "Here. A little housewarming gift."

I handed the bag to Cherie and she looked inside. "Oh, cool! It's that café painting we were looking at! This will be perfect in the kitchen."

She poked around the trunk and finally found a free spot where she could shove the bag. "We sure could use your truck. And it would be nice if you came along, too." Cherie laughed, then froze at the look on my face.

"Sorry," she said, looking down.

"It's ok," I replied. "Maybe I can come next year."

Crystal smiled. "We'll save a spot for ya."

"Thanks." I hugged them each in turn, feeling awkward and somber, but what could I say? *I'm glad you're going off without me! Have tons of fun doing what I wish I could do, what I slaved over to earn, while I stay here in the smoggy, gross city!*

"Well...we better hit the road. Traffic, you know." Cherie smiled a little awkwardly. "We'll see you at Christmas, Lil."

"We'll miss you!" Crystal waved cheerily as she climbed in the passenger side. Both their parents came out of the house then, so I took it as my cue to leave.

As I drove down to Front Street, my fake cheery mood disappeared. All this time I thought I'd taken things so well, but I couldn't stop the bitter tears of disappointment and jealousy. Everyone would head off to a new start but me. My best friends would live in the house that we'd *all* picked out, using the furniture we'd *all* picked out and hanging the picture that we'd *all* picked out in their kitchen. I clenched the steering wheel tightly, trying to ward off my growing anger.

I pulled into the hospital parking lot and finally eased my death grip on the wheel. The hospital seemed dark and gloomy, totally loathsome. I hated that they'd put mom here.

Instantly, I felt ashamed. Mom worked so hard all her life to help me, and then she'd been crippled with this hideous disease. And here I sat, pouting because I couldn't go to college. I sighed as I opened the door and headed to the hospital foyer. How could I feel so much pity and resentment at the same time? At least Wes stayed. I could turn to him when I needed him.

"Hi mom." I walked into her room with a few wildflowers I'd managed to find down by the beach. She sat up, looking better than she did the last time I saw her. Her freshly washed hair fell in soft brown curls around her shoulders the way mine did. My heart leapt at the sight of her eating soup and looking so alert.

"Lily! I'm so glad to see you. Did you get some good sleep last night?"

I rolled my eyes good-naturedly. Even through all of this, mom had never stopped being a typical mom. "Yes, mom. I even took a shower too."

"Good girl!" Her eyes lit up with her melodic laugh. I laughed along with her, feeling hollow inside. Poor, sweet mom. I tried to concentrate on Wes, how glad I felt that he wanted to be with me. I'd wanted so badly to kiss him last night, but I'd already felt too forward just holding his hand like I did. But I remembered the feeling of him, his arms around me, his soft voice reassuring me. Wes made me feel good again, like there could actually be hope in our bleak surroundings.

"Earth to Lily. Hello! What's going on?" Mom broke into my thoughts. She sounded more curious than suspicious.

I turned back to her, trying to look casual. "Nothing."

"Nothing, eh?" she said slyly. "Is it that boy? Did you go see him?"

"*Mom!*"

"Lily, do you really think I'm so old that I can't remember what it's like to be in love?"

"I'm not in love," I replied. "It's just…oh geez…"

"Not in love? Really? Your face is all red."

I took a deep breath. I didn't know why I felt so awkward about this. Mom and I always told each other everything. But Wes…he'd become such a huge part of my life. My feelings for him were so different, so much deeper than anything I'd ever felt. But I couldn't *not* tell her…

"Yes, I saw him last night. I guess we're kind of…dating now."

Mom gave a funny little shriek and pointed to the awful chair. "Sit!"

I sat down beside her and noticed that her face looked flushed instead of pale. She leaned closer, her eyes lit with excitement.

"Tell me about him."

"He's my age," I replied, not really knowing what to say. "We met at school."

"Was he the boy you went surfing with?"

"Yeah." I smiled in spite of the way I felt. I suddenly noticed mom had tears in her eyes. "What's wrong? Do you need me to get the nurse?"

"I'm just happy, honey," she said. "I can tell he makes you a lot happier than those other boys you've dated. I'm glad he's there for you. And I'm glad you have something good in your life since you're stuck taking care of me."

"Mom…I don't feel stuck with you at all." I thought I'd felt pretty bad before, but I felt a thousand times worse now. I took her hand in mine as she pushed her food tray away.

"That's sweet, honey," she said tearfully. "But I know it's an awful lot of responsibility. Especially now, when you're supposed to be starting out on your own, going to college with your friends and enjoying your life."

I shrugged and smiled what I hoped was a convincing smile. "It's ok. I love you, mom. I don't mind being here with you." I realized I really meant it, too. Yes, I felt bitter about not going away to Parthin, but mom needed me, and I wouldn't leave her.

She smiled and then scooted closer, looking all business. "How long have you known this boy?"

"We've gone to school together for years, but we didn't really talk until the beach trip."

"When do I get to meet him?"

"Uhhh…" I hadn't really thought about that. It wasn't that I didn't want the two of them to meet. It just seemed like a serious move, and we'd only just held hands. Besides, I had no idea what his work schedule would be like with the Defense Department.

"It's ok, honey, just when you both have time," she replied. "I promise I won't show him your naked baby pictures. Or I'll try not to, anyway."

"*Mom!*"

She laughed and looked down at the flowers in her hand. I couldn't believe how different she looked today. I felt the tiniest ray of hope that she'd stay well enough until I could save up the money for the treatment. And then, if she got better, maybe I'd be able to make it for the second half of the year up in Parthin…

"These are beautiful, where did you get them?" Her remark cut into my thoughts.

"Just down by the beach. Pretty, aren't they?"

She nodded and grabbed her hospital cup. It wasn't much of a vase, but it worked, especially since all the ice melted. I took a deep breath, bracing myself for the argument I knew would come. Part of me didn't want to ask her again about what she'd said, but it drove me crazy. I needed answers. Now.

"Hey mom?"

"What?"

"I need to ask you something." I fidgeted nervously.

"Ok."

"What strange things were you talking about on Sunday? I need to know," I started. She reacted just how I thought she would. Her eyes became hollow and shuttered. She looked out the window with an almost fearful look on her face.

"I don't want to press you if you're not feeling up to it," I offered, "But I just saw some weird things on the news and Wes mentioned a recruit-"

She took in a sharp breath, stopping me mid-sentence. She looked towards the door like she expected someone to be sitting there, eavesdropping.

"A recruit? You can't be serious."

I shrugged, feeling totally confused. "Yeah…he said they're talking to all the guys our age. I thought it was weird because some guy from the Mainframe came to talk to me last night and told me how important it was for me to join up."

Her eyes grew huge. "He asked you to sign up for the war?"

I felt fear rising in the pit of my stomach, just as it did when I talked to Wes the night before. "Yeah…"

"Oh no," she moaned as she buried her head in her hands.

"What? What's wrong?"

She lifted her head and looked around. "I just can't believe they're starting…they said it would be months, maybe even years!"

She looked hysterical, and seemed to be talking more to herself than me.

"Wes said something about the war, that they've already shipped troops," I said cautiously.

Her eyes widened. "They have?"

"Yeah."

"I had my suspicions, but they really…" She trailed off, lost in thought. I grabbed her hand gently.

"Mom, what's going on? You know something, what is it?"

She pressed her lips tightly together and looked away. "Don't worry about it, Lily."

"What?" I jumped up, my voice rising. "What do you mean, don't worry about it? How can you just say that when you're completely freaking out about whatever it is?"

She looked back at me, and my heart sank as I watched shadows form under her eyes again. Her healthy glow from earlier slowly disappeared.

"We are *not* talking about it, Lily. I don't want you to ever mention the war again, do you understand me?"

I stepped back a little, my mind whirling with shock. "But why?"

"Just promise me, Lily. Don't ask me again." I'd rarely seen mom like this, completely set and determined. She usually caved when I begged for what I wanted, but I knew not to argue when she got that look.

"Ok," I said dejectedly. "I promise."

Chapter Thirteen

"Lily, are you ok?" Wes looked at me expectantly.

I shook myself out of my stupor. He smiled down at me, making my heart speed up a notch. "Yeah, sorry…just lost in thought," I replied.

This past week I'd spent more and more time with Wes. He stayed present in my thoughts almost every minute of the day. A little unnerving, but how can I not think of him? I'd never been with anyone who felt so concerned with what I wanted, what I thought. We spent hours just talking about the past, our childhoods, our plans for the future. Even though he had to work for the Defense Department, he wanted more than anything to work with animals.

I'd even met his family one night when he invited me for dinner. His mom hugged and fussed over me immediately, but his dad didn't say a word to me.

Wes also came with me to the hospital a couple times to visit mom. I'd thought it would feel weird, introducing him to mom, but they hit it off immediately. While he worked, I spent time with mom in the hospital. As soon as visiting hours ended, we spent our time at the beach, watching the sunset, surfing or just taking walks while we held hands.

But everything's changing today, now that I would take Wes's place at the Ration Center. I'd work several hours, and Wes's schedule would be hectic. It would be hard to see each other between work and hospital visits.

Wes opened his mouth to reply, but the manager of the Ration Center, and my future boss, started talking. Gerald filled the room with his big, beefy presence. A ring of dark hair wound around his bald head, accompanied by a huge mustache that ruffled every time he talked. I thought it seemed kind of gross that this big, sweaty guy organized food distribution for the whole city, but he seemed nice enough.

"We're glad to have you, Lily," he said. "Wes told me you'll do great here and I hope he's right. You've got some big shoes to fill."

Yeah, like I didn't know already. Everyone obviously wanted him to stay. He shrugged modestly, then rolled his eyes at me when Gerald looked away. I bit back a laugh as a couple other workers motioned us toward the door of the huge depot. Wes would act as my trainer for today and then I'd start work full time in the morning while he started at the Department of Defense.

"This is where we keep all the food," Gerald explained. "The warehouse is organized into different sections, each housing grains, legumes and perishables. Orders brought to us by patrons are to be strictly followed. We can't hand out extras or make exceptions for anyone, or that's all we'll hear about from the Fooders at the Mainframe."

"What's a Fooder?" I whispered to Wes.

"Guys at the Rations Department at the Mainframe."

"Oh."

"Right, Wes, I gotta fill out some invoices, think you can handle it from here?" Gerald looked at Wes expectantly.

"Yeah, that should be fine."

"Thanks, bud."

"Alone at last," Wes whispered slyly to me.

I turned bright red, making Gerald look at me questioningly. I pushed Wes playfully when Gerald turned around and started walking.

"You're in big trouble for that one," I whispered.

"Ooh, bring it on." He grinned down at me devilishly, and I pushed him again a little harder.

Gerald walked away into a different corridor, talking to some of the other workers. Wes showed me around the huge storerooms, the office and the break room. After that, he showed me how to fill out a transport order, a walk-in order and a Communicator order, or Com for short. I'd been to the Ration Center before to get food, but it was very different seeing everything from the inside.

"And finally, don't give anyone more than they have money for or else the Fooders will chop our heads off and put them up on display in the Mainframe for other dissenters. And that's about it. Piece of cake."

Wes laughed as my eyes got big. "Just kidding!" he yelled as I started jabbing him. He grabbed me around the waist, pinning my arms to his sides to keep me from poking him. As his laughter died down, he smiled at me, his eyes intense. My heart began beating out of control.

"All right, you two, enough PDA," said Gerald as he walked into the room. We broke apart quickly. "Did you give her the tour? Or have you just been making out all this time?"

"Yeah, Big G, I did. Relax."

I looked from Gerald to Wes, thinking surely Wes would be chewed out for talking back, but Gerald just laughed a big, deep laugh that shook his belly.

"All right, then, we need you to work to the end of the shift. Lily, work with Wes today so we can see what you're made of. You'll be in charge of filling Com orders."

"You ready?" Wes grabbed my hand and smiled.

"Yeah. Piece of cake, right?"

"Right."

For the rest of the evening, we filled orders as people's faces popped up on the huge communicator screens. I didn't know why Gerald and Wes kept warning me not to give anyone more than their money's worth, but I soon learned why. Everyone in the country owned Mainframe-issued communicators, little devices that contained built-in video phones and access to the main database of information. The Mainframe controlled all distribution of information on the communicators, and people could put in food orders through the Food Distribution channel. People who made less income tried to adjust their orders to get more food, or tried to adjust the amount of money in their account, but the Mainframe controlled all the money in order to prevent things like fraud or counterfeit that people did in old days.

"You have to be careful," Wes said after a particularly difficult order in which a man tried to get more than his allotted amount of grain. His thin, pale face startled me. He looked awful, completely starved. "People will try anything."

"We have a ton of food." I couldn't believe how little each person got. Mom and I had always had enough to meet our needs, but people with families twice or even three times our size didn't get much more than we did. "Why all the stinginess?"

"It's not stinginess, Lily. It's necessary." His voice lowered deeply until I could barely hear it. "We can't grow food anymore, and the Fooders are breaking their necks trying to figure out how to get more once this lot runs out. It's probably another reason the Mainframe is starting this stupid war."

"What do you mean?"

"I mean, the Southern Province has plenty of food. They figured out how to clean the soil, so they can still grow things."

"What do you mean 'clean the soil?' I thought it was *their* fault our soil was faulty."

"That's what the Mainframe tells us, but it's not true. Haven't you ever heard of the Burial?"

Something hovered on the edge of my memory, but I couldn't quite place it. I thought of Mr. Allen again. He'd told us something about all this...but what?

"What's the Burial?"

"I can't talk about it here." He looked around, fear in his eyes. "I'll tell you next time we're at the beach."

"But how do you know about all of this?"

"The Subversive, remember?" he muttered.

I looked at him for a long moment, surprised at his solemn face. He turned back to the screen as another order popped up. I wanted badly to ask him more, but I couldn't. Bringing up underground movements would be a bad idea in a Mainframe warehouse. We filled it quickly, sorted the items and put them in a box as Gerald walked in the room.

"I think that wraps it up for the night," he said, his mustache ruffling. "We'll see you tomorrow at nine then, Lily?"

"Yeah, I'll be here."

"All right then," he replied. "Wes, we'll miss you. Good luck."

They shook hands, then Gerald typed in the amount of Wes's last paycheck on his communicator. He left, and we followed him through the halls as the lights shut off. We dropped off our last order at the loading docks and headed for the main lobby.

"Do you want me to take you home?" said Wes.

"It's ok, I don't live too far from here. I didn't even drive."

"But...it's getting dark out." His eyebrows creased with worry.

I rolled my eyes. "I'll be fine. It's summer. The sun won't go down for another couple hours. Just get yourself home, you're probably starving."

He struggled for a moment, then gently took my hands in his. "I'm really worried about you being in your apartment alone while your mom's in the hospital."

"I'll be fine, Wes. That's sweet of you to worry about me."

I squeezed his hand and smiled but it didn't wash away the concern on his face.

"What time do you get off work tomorrow?" I asked.

"I'm not sure. It's orientation, so I'll give you a call and let you know. If it's not too late, maybe we can go to the beach."

"Ok. Sounds great."

He wrapped his arms me, his shoulders tense. "Why don't we take our rations and go eat in the park?" he said suddenly. "We haven't really had a first date, you have to admit."

"Yes we did!" I looked at him indignantly.

"You kept blowing me off and insisting that other people come with us."

"Yeah, but we've been to the beach plenty of times on our own," I argued back.

"But we never planned it. This is planned."

I frowned at him, then laughed. "Ok, fine. If it will make you feel better, we can go to the park and eat our dinner together before you take me home."

He smiled, obviously relieved, and took my hand as we headed out the doors. Clouds gathered, blocking out the sun and making everything a little darker and more ominous. Suddenly I felt glad to have Wes there with me. I gripped his hand a little more tightly as we walked to his car.

The street seemed relatively quiet when we left the Ration Center, but I noticed a slight tapping noise behind me. Footsteps.

"Wes, someone is following us," I whispered as quietly as I could. He nodded very slightly and pulled me closer to his side. Worry covered his face again.

We got to the car and Wes hurried to open my door for me, but a voice behind us made him stop.

"Pardon me, but are you Lily Mitchell?" The voice spoke sharply, as if the speaker usually barked orders instead of chatting casually. I turned to see a man with a sallow face and eerie eyes staring at me. His eyes…they flashed the same way as the creepy parking attendant, the Mainframe guy, even the nasty substitute teacher.

"Who wants to know?" I sounded much braver than I felt.

"I've just heard a lot about you," he said, smiling. His crooked brown teeth made my stomach turn. That same horrible, nightmarish feeling I'd gotten from the others crept into my gut, churning out every awful memory I'd ever had, but this guy seemed a thousand times worse than any of them. I could barely stand next to him without feeling like my heart would explode from fear.

"Are you from the Mainframe? Because I've already told you people I'm not joining up!" My voice rose steadily until I nearly shouted.

He laughed, probably meaning to sound casual, but it came out more like a harsh cough. Who is this guy? Why did I always run into people with a disturbing interest in me?

"No, I'm not from the Mainframe. Not anymore," he said. He rolled his eyes and smirked. "But I think I know everything I need to know now. Have a nice day."

He walked away, still laughing. Wes opened the door and practically shoved me into the car. He'd barely shut my door when he bolted for the driver's side and climbed in frantically.

"What was *that* all about?" he panted as he fumbled with the key card.

"I don't know," I replied, shaking all over. "But I think I'm being followed."

Chapter Fourteen

"What are you talking about?" Wes could hardly slide the key card into the slot of his car. I grabbed his hand firmly and helped him get the key in. The car revved to life as the computer components aligned with the engine. Wes hurriedly tapped the shift screen and pushed his finger down hard on drive. His little car shot forward and down the street.

"I...I don't know, I can't think here," I stuttered, my heart still racing. "Can we go to the beach instead of the park?"

Wes looked confused for a moment before he finally gathered himself. He changed course without a word, his brow deeply furrowed. I stared out at the landscape flying by. The grimy city buildings gradually gave way to the large forest that bordered the highway. Mom's strange warning floated through my consciousness. Why would she say something like that? The stories about beasts weren't true. They couldn't be...could they?

Wes pulled up to a deserted cove and took out the key card. His hands shook slightly as he grabbed our food and opened his door. He walked around the car and opened my door for me.

"What's going on?" he asked when we finally settled near the water.

"I don't know, but people keep following me everywhere and telling me to join up for the war."

"But that guy didn't say anything about the war, and he's not from the Mainframe."

He stood up and ran a hand through his hair distractedly. His face was pale, drawn, worried.

"Why would they want you so bad?"

I shrugged. "My mom knows something, but she won't tell me. She told me never bring it up again."

He sat down again, drumming his fingers restlessly. "That guy...there was something totally wrong about him. I mean, did you feel..."

He stopped talking abruptly. I knew why. It seemed so ridiculous to admit. How could a person make you feel that way? Just by standing next to you?

"Yes," I said quietly. "I felt horrible, like someone injected me with poison or something. I've never felt anything like it."

He let out a long breath. "How could someone do that? It's not normal."

"I don't know." We sat in troubled silence for a long time. I couldn't think of what to say or do. I ground my teeth, totally frustrated. Wes probably felt the same way. With nothing else to do, we ate our sandwiches and stared out at the waves.

After a while, Wes perked up. "Your mom."

"What?"

"Your mom, Lil. You said she knows something."

I rolled my eyes. "Yeah, she does, but she made me swear on my first born child that I'd never talk about it again. And when she says no, she means it. Trust me."

"But what if I went with you? Maybe she'd be more willing to talk if I was there."

"What makes you so special? I'm her daughter, and she won't tell me anything" I scoffed.

"Then what do you want to do?"

I let out an exasperated sigh. "Ok, fine, we can give it a try. I haven't talked to her yet today, anyway. But I don't think she'll say anything."

"Come on." Wes stood up, grabbed my hand and headed towards his car. We got back to the hospital in record time, just fifteen minutes before visiting hours were to end.

Mom sat up watching the news as we walked in, but she clicked off the screen as soon as she saw us.

"Wes, Lily! I wondered if you two would stop by-"

"Mrs. Mitchell, I'm sorry to cut you off, but we really need to know something before the staff kicks us out," Wes interrupted.

She looked taken aback for a moment, then narrowed her eyes. "What?"

Wes hurriedly explained what happened with the creepy man when we left the Ration Center. Mom's expression went from worried, to terrified, to sick.

"What did he look like again?" she whispered.

"He was just odd. His eyes were really scary. He just looked like he could kill someone."

"He was really pale, too," I chimed in. "Like, freakishly pale."

Mom's expression, if possible, got worse. She covered her eyes with her hands. "I knew this would happen eventually…I just didn't think it would be so soon."

I sat down on one of the awful chairs, and Wes followed. "Mom, I've got to know what's going on. People keep following us, and I'm afraid they'll get so anxious to find me that they'll go after you."

She sighed deeply. "You're right.

I sat back. "About what?"

She took a deep, shaky breath. "They do have a reason for coming after you."

A huge lump formed in my throat. "Why?"

"Your father was involved in something the Mainframe has been hushing up for almost twenty years. He was one of the original Innovators."

"Um…what?"

She frowned. "Haven't you learned about Innovators in history?"

"No," I replied, completely confused, but Wes looked furious.

"You mean the idiots who did the Burial wrong and then just left before they could take the heat?" he muttered angrily. I looked at him, shocked. I'd never seen him so mad about anything. Mom's cheeks grew red.

"They didn't just run off," she shot back. "They were run off by the Mainframe."

"Why would the Mainframe run them off? They were supposed to be put on trial."

"My husband," said mom, her voice rising, "was an Innovator. And yes, something went wrong with the Burial, but the Mainframe didn't want to pay for better materials to bury with!"

"Whoa, time out!" I yelled, holding up my hands. "Your husband, as in my dad?"

"Yes." She stared at Wes, still stony-faced.

"Hold on, what exactly did they bury?"

"Radioactive material," Wes put in. "They didn't need it anymore."

"Radioactive…you mean like the stuff that people used to build bombs with in old days?" I vaguely remembered reading something about that in science class.

"Yes," Mom said again. "They discovered something called Akrium, which could build much more efficient bombs than the old A-bombs. So they decided to bury the old radioactive materials, but…they did it wrong. The ruined soil caused our current famine."

A light bulb flashed on in my head. "Mr. Allen…"

"Who?" asked mom, but Wes nodded.

"Yeah, he tried to tell us that the Mainframe was wrong, that we were responsible for the soil pollution, but the school went berserk and fired him when they found out."

I remembered now. He'd just up and left, and they'd told us all he was going on sabbatical for his sanity. They lied. Who else had lied? What else had the Mainframe covered up?

"Ok, now we know all about the history of bombs, but what does any of this have to do with me?" I said, waving my hands as if to clear the confusion in my brain.

"They also found out that Akrium could alter DNA and make a person practically…indestructible. The Mainframe Defense Department decided to try to use it to build up an army of invincible soldiers instead of bombs. Those Innovators were in the first testing group, and things went *horribly* wrong."

"What happened?"

Mom's eyes became distant again as she turned to stare out the window. "They mutated."

"What?" It sounded ridiculous, like one of those old comic books people used to read so much. I laughed a little. "Stuff like that doesn't happen, mom. That's crazy!"

I started to laugh again, and Wes too, but mom's face didn't change. She still wore a stoic mask, but I could see a deep sadness in her eyes. She turned back to me, gazing steadily at me with her sunken eyes.

"It did happen. Some reacted to the injection faster than others. They turned into beast-like things. Their skin turned all pale and they lost their hair. Some even lost their minds. They became nearly indestructible, but they'd also become monsters."

An awful, icy fist clenched around my stomach. "So…you mean all those stories you used to tell me…"

"They're true, Lily," she replied. "They weren't just a bedtime story. Beasts *do* live in the woods south of the city. The Mainframe would have executed them. They ran and hid. No one has seen them since."

My head spun, making me feel like I would pass out any second. I'd always thought those stories were more of a cautionary tale, something mom told me to keep me from wandering too far. And her description…it sounded like the man we'd met on the street. I looked over at Wes. His expression mirrored what I thought.

"So that guy on the street, was he…"

Mom nodded solemnly. "If he said he used to work for the Mainframe, I think he *is* a beast."

Chapter Fifteen

I wondered if mom's drugs kicked in. That had to be it. Her story felt too ridiculous to be real. Beasts walking around disguised as people? Following me?

But her gaunt appearance pretty much confirmed that it wasn't a joke, or a hallucination. I knew her too well. She wouldn't make up something like this.

"How do you know?" I finally asked.

"Your father was one of those scientists, remember? He was an Innovator."

I stared at her, wide eyed. "So…you're saying dad turned into a *monster*? That he lives in the trees? And that's why he hasn't been around my whole life?" I started looking for the call button, but mom caught me. She grabbed the call button and held it tightly in her hand.

"Listen to me, Lily," she rasped. I drew in a sharp breath, startled by the hard, flashing look in her eyes. "I know I sound crazy, but this is serious!"

I sat back, stunned. "Your father didn't react to the Akrium as fast as the others did. The Mainframe realized what happened and tried to cover it up. They tried to shoot the scientists, but they underestimated the beast's power. They had nowhere to go but the woods."

"Well, if they ran away, how did you know about dad?" I asked.

"He came to see me one last time after it-"

"Wait a minute," I interrupted. "Weren't you totally terrified of him? You said they all turned into *beasts*."

"They did, Lily, but I said that your father reacted slower than the others. He looked pale and his eyes flashed in a weird way, but he didn't seem much different besides that. He told me he would soon be like the others. He didn't have much time, but he wanted to say goodbye."

"So he just said goodbye and left? Nice," I muttered. I'd never known much about dad, but hearing this didn't impress me much or make me feel closer to him. I looked up at mom. Tears filled her eyes as she looked down at the old wedding band she always wore.

"Lily, I know I haven't given you the best picture of your father, but we did love each other very much. I've never said much about him because I was scared."

"Of what?"

She closed her eyes, breathing deep to steady herself. "I didn't want you knowing too much because I knew someday the Mainframe would come for you. That's why I wanted you to drop it the last time you asked me about it."

I laughed again, a short unfeeling laugh of shock. "Why would the Mainframe come after me?"

"That night your father came…it was our last night together." She looked away to stare out of the window again. "After he left, I realized I was pregnant with you."

I stared at her for a moment as the news sank in. "Ok…but still, what does all this have to do with the Mainframe?"

"They never gave up on Akrium injections. They tried several different chemical combinations to create indestructible soldiers without the side effects, but pretty much all of the experiments failed. The subjects who didn't fully mutate just disappeared. I'm sure the Mainframe suspected the beasts for the disappearances, but of course they couldn't tell the public that."

"So…" I prompted. "Why would they come for me?"

"Don't you understand, Lily?" She looked at me again, exasperated. "Your father had *already been injected* with the Akrium when I got pregnant with you. It makes a person almost completely immune to disease or harm."

"Ok…" I felt stupid and slow. She looked at me like my trig teacher used to, completely exasperated that I couldn't calculate a trajectory.

"You *have* the properties of Akrium in you. Without the side effects."

"So? Why would the Mainframe care?"

"You *are* the perfect soldier that they've been trying to create all these years!" she said, throwing her hands up in the air. "Haven't you ever wondered why you never get sick? Why you've never had a serious injury that lasted a long time? Why you're good at every sport you've ever played?"

And suddenly, I realized she wasn't crazy. Mainframe doctors discovered the cure for things like colds and sore throats and even most cancers long ago, but some of the tougher strains of disease still existed. And yet, I'd hardly ever stayed home sick from school. I'd always been really good at sports. And Wes even thought it was strange that I'd walked away from near drowning that day at the beach…

"Oh. That's why they're trying to recruit me." It wasn't a question, just a blunt statement. The puzzle pieces fell grimly into place, sealing my horrible fate.

"I always worried that it might be true, but now I *know* it's true. I'm sure they did the math and realized you were born nine months after the mutation. They've probably had their eyes on you for a long time now, monitoring everything you do."

The thought made me dizzy and sick. All the weird people I'd seen in the past couple weeks, the man on the cliff, the creepy parking attendant, the man in the garage…had they all been sent to spy on me? Were they beasts? Mainframe officials? Both?

"Why haven't they come for me sooner?"

She shrugged. "It's just my theory, but I think they wanted to wait until you were considered an official adult before they made any moves. You wouldn't have been much use as a kid or even a young teenager."

"What about the guy on the street?" Wes asked. I jumped a little. I'd forgotten that he sat right next to me. Mom's eyes grew fearfully large.

"I didn't bank on that," she whispered, her voice constricted with fear. "But the beasts must have found out about you. They're probably after you too, because you might be the means of a cure."

I stood up, terrified, furious, nauseated. "So I'm doomed? I'm either going to be drafted into a war to go kill people, or get captured by freaks who live in the woods?"

"Lily, calm down!" Mom's face shimmered with tears, but I barely noticed. *I'm a mutant, tainted by something I have no control over.*

Bitter tears of rage, embarrassment, shame washed down my face. I ran out of the room, down the hall, through the front doors, down the street. I kept running, only tiring a little. No wonder I'd been the best runner on the track team. *After all*, I thought desperately, *I am half-beast forest freak.*

I made it through the slums, up Front street, past the gigantic Mainframe building and finally out onto the cliffs. It had to have been at least four miles, but I didn't care. I didn't stop as I took the cliff path onto the sand. I finally sank down at the end of the small pier that jutted out into the water, sobbing and panting uncontrollably. I must have run for at least twenty minutes or so. I felt bad enough knowing what I was, why they wanted me, but it felt way worse knowing that Wes heard it all. No way would he stick around now.

I finally wiped away the last of my tears and stared out at the waves, feeling numb. A hand suddenly gripped my shoulder and I screamed. I tore myself away and stood up, ready to fight if I had to. Wes stood there, his face a strange mixture of relief and terror.

"How did you get here?" he gasped. "I've been looking everywhere, the hospital, your apartment, the park…"

He trailed off, trying to catch his breath. I didn't answer, just burst into tears again. I wrapped my arms around his waist and buried my face in his shoulder. I don't know how long he held me and let me cry. I didn't care. He stood there, not running away, something I could hold onto while I fell apart.

I finally stopped crying and looked up at him. He leaned his forehead against mine.

"Why does life have to be a constant hell?" I muttered.

His expression confused me. I couldn't tell if he pitied me or if he struggled to think of an answer. Maybe both.

"It doesn't always have to be hell," he finally said. His hands moved to my waist and pulled me closer to him. Slowly, he brushed his lips against mine and pulled back, his face a mix of fear and hope.

I'd kissed boys before, but I'd never felt anything quite like this. Something exploded inside me. His hands moved from my hips to my back, pulling me in until we were so close we practically became one person. My arms circled his neck, pulling him to me, suddenly frantic that I would lose him too.

Our lips met again in a collision of fire, both of us unleashing the feelings that lingered so deep for so long. For the first time in a long time, I felt alive. I felt real. The chaos in my brain subsided, leaving only the bliss of the moment.

Chapter Sixteen

The moon rose high in the inky sky by the time Wes dropped me off at my apartment. He insisted on walking me to the door. Honestly, it felt good to have someone who felt so concerned about me. Mom loved me and worried about me, but I worried about her every second of every day and it got a bit taxing sometimes.

"You're sure you'll be ok?" He looked around uncertainly.

"I'm sure." I smiled at him shyly, the memory of our intense kiss still fresh in my mind. "Thank you for everything."

He smiled and brushed his fingers against my cheek before leaning in for a quick, sweet peck. "I'll call you before I go to work at nine. Is that too early?"

"No, it's ok, I need to go to work by ten. I'll be up." I kissed his cheek and hugged him. "I'll see you in the morning then."

"Yeah," he replied. "I won't forget. Lock your door."

I rolled my eyes. "Yes, mom."

He laughed and squeezed my hand. "Good night, Lily."

"Goodnight."

With one last smile, he left, walked down the stairs and into the garage. I waited for the reassuring sound of his car. He pulled out of the garage and headed up the street to his neighborhood on the cliffs. I looked longingly after him until I couldn't see him anymore, then stepped into my apartment and bolted the door.

As soon as I got inside, I wished he'd stayed with me. The apartment felt so empty. I missed mom more than ever. I turned on the air, went through my usual nightly routine and settled down in my covers. Just as I started to drift off, I heard a low click from the front room. My eyes shot open and I lay there, rigid, in the dark. I could barely hear a slight shuffling noise, followed by the sound of distant footsteps on the stairs.

I sat up, sweat breaking out on my forehead and neck. Someone stood at the door just a minute ago. I couldn't move, but I had to see who had come.

Finally, my heart pounding in my ears, I got out of bed and flew through the hallway to the front room. A white envelope sat in front of the door. Someone had just pushed it through the mail slot. I knelt next to the white square and picked it up gingerly. I wondered wildly if it might be a bomb. My fingers started to tremble when I saw the Mainframe insignia stamped in the corner.

I got up quickly and ran to the window that faced the street. The low rumble of an engine sounded as a car slithered silently out of the parking garage. I could barely make out the Mainframe decals on the license plate as it drove through a patch of moonlight. I thought of the creepy man who'd been in the parking garage that night, how he promised one day I would join the troops one way or another. A terrible shiver crept up my spine.

I hurried back to the envelope and tore it open:

To Miss Lily Mitchell:

You have received this letter as a summons to the Defense Department of the Mainframe on Saturday the 13th of July. You are asked to arrive no later than 8:30 am. This is not a request. Failure to appear for this appointment will result in severe penalty.

Regards,

Victor Channing, Head of Defense

I read the letter again and again, hardly daring to believe what I saw. My head swam as I tried to remember where I'd heard the name before. Not at school, or from mom. Then it hit me.

The news. Victor Channing, the oily man on TV that night in the hospital. The one who'd announced the war. Why did I have to see him? What did they mean, a "severe penalty?" How did they know everything about me and keep track of me?

I slumped to the floor, close to tears. Maybe I could run, and take mom with me. But even as I started to feel hope, I realized I couldn't take mom far from the hospital. Even if I got her to another hospital, the doctors and nurses wouldn't know her condition and history.

It suddenly struck me how old I felt. My eighteenth birthday loomed close, but I felt thirty, or even fifty. I'd felt this way since mom got sick. Every muscle in my body ached, my head pounded.

Not knowing what else to do, I looked at the letter again. July thirteenth, my birthday. Maybe that had something to do with it. Like mom said, they waited until I became an official adult.

I rubbed my eyes and thought about work the next day. I'd get off at five, and hospital visiting hours didn't end until eight. Maybe mom would know what to do, or figure out how to get out of it. I finally climbed back in bed, feeling a little nauseous as I drifted off into an uneasy sleep.

The next day grew hot and muggy through the morning, and I thought longingly of the beach. What I wouldn't give to surf all day in the cold water without a care in the world. I tried not to think about the letter as I showered, got dressed and put on a little makeup. My communicator rang just as I poured myself a bowl of cereal.

"Hey beautiful," said Wes as his face popped up on the screen.

"Hello yourself, handsome," I said with a smile. "Don't you have to leave for work soon?"

The clock read ten to nine. He shrugged, scowling slightly. "Yeah. I'm leaving in a few minutes, but I don't live too far from the main building."

"Oh, ok."

He shrugged and smiled. "How are you?"

"Tired, but good."

"Did I keep you up too late? If I did, just remember it was your idea to go running off to the beach."

I laughed and shook my head. "No…I just didn't sleep too well."

His smile melted instantly into concern. "Why?"

I took a deep breath, then told him about the strange letter I'd gotten last night. His frown grew deeper and deeper the more I talked until he looked like he would seriously hurt someone.

"Lily, you've got to hide!" he burst out when I finished. "You can't go to this summons, it could be a trap!"

I smiled wryly. "If they wanted me that bad, I think they'd just knock me over the head and shove me in one of their fancy cars instead of leaving me a note."

"I wouldn't put it past them," he muttered darkly. Suddenly, a look of fear crossed his face. I understood why. Conversations on communicators were usually watched.

"Tell you what, can I pick you up after work? I get off at four-thirty and I know you get off at five," he offered.

"Well, I planned on going to see mom…you can come if you like."

"Ok, I'll meet you at your work," he replied. "I can chat with some of the guys while I wait for you."

"Ok, I'll see you then."

"See you later."

I clicked the off button and stowed my communicator in my back pocket. Thankfully, the parking garage remained empty as I crept down to my truck. I didn't live far from work, but I felt too scared to walk today. My faithful old truck took a while to start, making me nervous as I glanced out the window. I loved my car, but sometimes I wished it started faster. It didn't have the computerized shift or a key card. It had an old key, a long piece of plastic made to fit the ignition, but it didn't have a ridged metal prong like the car keys from years and years ago.

Then engine finally roared to life and I peeled out of the garage towards work. I rolled down my windows and tried to relax as I breathed in the warm air. I didn't have a lot to do at work, and by the time lunch rolled around I wanted to get out of the hot warehouse. I took my lunch to the nearby park where Wes and I were supposed to go the other night. I settled on a bench and relaxed. I could almost forget about all the weird things that happened as I ate in the sunshine.

I enjoyed my lunch until I noticed a strange man on a bench not too far away. He wore really dark sunglasses, his skin pale against the bright sun. I couldn't tell if he watched me, but his head had turned in my direction. He didn't move, just kept staring through those sunglasses. I finally got up and walked to my car, trying not to look nervous. As I climbed in my front seat, I looked out the window covertly to see what he did. His head swiveled slowly towards my car, coming to a stop as soon as he faced me.

Chapter Seventeen

My heart nearly exploded as I turned my key and revved the engine to life. Another beast. Within two days. What if *they* watched me round the clock too? Who else followed me? What did they want? All these thoughts tumbled through my mind non-stop as I flew through the streets of the city, navigating around the noon-time traders and beggars. My breathing didn't slow until I pulled into the warehouse parking lot.

"What's wrong, Lily?" Gerald looked at me, his eyebrows raised in alarm. "You look like you've seen a ghost!"

I gave a weak laugh instead of answering. What could I say? A mutant freak sat and watched me in the park?

I ran quickly to the back room and started work, trying desperately to keep my mind off the man in the park. The time passed quickly and soon I stood in the main lobby with Gerald, waiting while he typed in my hours and pay for the day on my communicator.

"You sure you're ok? You looked really scared when you came in." He seemed genuinely worried. I felt a rush of gratitude towards him.

"Yeah…thanks, Gerald. I'm all right."

He raised his eyebrows questioningly, but Wes walked through the door just at that moment. I gave Gerald a quick smile and ran towards him. He noticed that I shook slightly as he pulled me into his arms.

"What's wrong?" he asked, looking me over urgently like he expected to find an open wound.

"I'll tell you on the way."

We hurried out the doors to his car. He'd parked beside me, so we decided to take my car back to my apartment before heading to the hospital. Soon we sat side by side in his little car, driving up Front Street to see mom.

"So what happened?" he asked.

"I saw another beast at the park today at lunch."

"*What?*" Wes's face twisted into a stark combination of terror and fury.

"He didn't do anything. He just stared at me, but it scared me pretty bad."

He shook his head disgustedly. "How do these guys just walk around? You'd think someone would notice the creepers."

"They must have a way to disguise themselves, like mom said," I replied. I shivered slightly, remembering the man that stopped Wes and I on the street. Something about him looked *wrong*, like a rag doll hastily pieced together.

Wes sighed deeply as he turned the corner into the hospital parking lot. "Lily, you've got to get out of this city. Take your mom with you."

"I've thought about that, Wes, but even if I could take her somewhere with a hospital, the doctors wouldn't know her or her history."

"What are you going to do about the summons?"

"I have to go, don't I?" I paused, trying to collect my thoughts as I stared out the window. "I don't know. I wanted to see what my mom said."

"You know she'll be worried."

I let out an impatient huff of breath. "I know, but I don't know what else to do. I can't just ignore it and pretend it's not there. Mom knows more about the Mainframe than most people. She'll know what to do."

With that, Wes turned off the car and slid the keycard into his pocket. We climbed out and headed to the doors. Most of the staff knew us well by now and waved hello.

We got to mom's room and knocked. She called for us to come in, sounding a little strained. She sat up in bed, eating dinner and looking a little paler than the last time I saw her. I knew immediately that something happened. She forced a smile and motioned for us to sit down.

"Hi, love. How are you, Wes?"

Wes smiled back. "Hi, Mrs. Mitchell."

Mom took one more bite of her toast, then slid her tray away half-eaten. "Ugh…hospital food," she said, pretending to gag.

A horrible guilt rose within me. She already looked like she harbored bad news, and I came to deliver more.

"Lily?"

"Hmm?" I glanced up, startled.

"I asked you how work went today." Mom looked at me expectantly, the uneasiness more present in her eyes. Wes sat down on one of the chairs and gently pulled me into the seat next to me.

"Oh…fine," I replied. I tried my best to keep my expression light, but mom saw through it in a second.

"What's wrong, honey?"

I fidgeted nervously. "I got…a summons. From the Mainframe."

All the color drained from her face. "No."

"They left a letter in the mail slot last night. I…I don't know what to do about it."

Mom leaned back against her pillows, a slight sweat breaking on her forehead. "The man who came to the house that day…he warned me they would get you one way or the other. And now they have."

"That's what they told me too, but I never thought they were serious" I whispered, my heart dropping into my stomach. I grabbed her hand, hoping she wouldn't slip into another fit of hysterics like the one that landed her in the hospital in the first place.

"We can't let it happen," said Wes in a deep, hushed voice. "Why don't we get you out of here, Elaine? You and Lily can skip town, hide for a while until the heat dies down and this dumb war is over."

Mom's lip began to tremble. "I can't give Lily the burden of caring for me. I…"

She trailed off as she slipped into silent sobs. Wes bit his lip, looking guilty. He reached for my arm and squeezed it gently.

"I'll head out and find something for us to eat in the cafeteria," he said meaningfully. I nodded mutely, still scared by mom's reaction. He left the room and I scooted closer to her.

"Lily," she murmured, "the doctor talked to me this morning. I can't run away with you honey. It just wouldn't work."

Boiling lava trickled into my stomach, making me nauseous and weak all over. I knew what she'd say before she even said it.

"They said you're terminal, didn't they?" The words choked in my throat.

She nodded slowly, tears glazing her cheeks. "The only cure at this point is the Barbach treatment."

Overwhelmed, I buried my face in my hands, hoping somehow the news would disappear, cease to exist. I wanted to shake it out of my ears, make it so I never heard it. Mom didn't have any time left. I had to get the money *now.* But how?

"How long did they give you?" I croaked.

"Two months. Maybe less."

The words hung in the air like an awful cloud of doom, casting its dark shadow over everything it touched. I'd never save up enough in time. I stood up and paced angrily, completely helpless, but I couldn't just sit around and do nothing. *The doctors,* I thought savagely, *they have to do something. It's their job!*

"NO! They will find a cure if they have to work all night!" I shouted, clutching her hand tightly.

"Lily, there's nothing more they can do."

I pushed the chair over, lost in a fit of rage. "NO! THEY WILL FIND A CURE! I'M NOT LOSING YOU!"

I knew I sounded psychotic, but I didn't care. Wes ran in, along with some nurses. I knew they tried to calm me, but everything seemed to swirl together strangely. Their words blurred around me nonsensically, making me sicker by the minute.

Finally, I crumpled to the floor, wanting to die, wanting to leave this miserable place. If mom left, I couldn't stay behind. In the flurry of voices and pain, my world slowly faded to black.

Chapter Eighteen

I woke up ready to puke. My vision slowly cleared and I saw Wes sitting beside me. I sat up and looked around, confused. I laid in my bed, in my room.

"You were pretty hysterical," said Wes quietly. "Your mom and the doctors agreed that it would be better to get you home."

"What time is it?" My voice sounded croaky, unnatural.

"Midnight." His usual goofy grin had long disappeared, making him look gaunt and a little ill.

I scooted up against the pillows. "Is mom ok?"

He nodded and tried to stifle a yawn. "She was worried about you, but wanted you home. But she asked if I could bring you by tomorrow sometime, since it's your birthday and all."

I felt a funny twinge. I'd completely forgotten about my birthday. With a sickening lurch in my stomach, I remembered that I had to go to the summons too. Mom had never told me what I needed to do.

"The letter!" I cried. "I have to go to the Mainframe in the morning by 8:30!"

He creased his eyebrows. "Can't you reschedule? I mean, you're sick. You have an excuse."

"Wes, this isn't school anymore. I don't have a choice," I muttered. Happy birthday to me.

"Let's not worry about that now," he whispered. His eyes filled with sympathy as he took my hand. "I'm so sorry about your mom, Lily. If I had the money I would give it to you in a heartbeat."

"I know you would." Tears threatened to choke me again. I sat up and leaned gently against him. He started stroking my hair.

"What are we going to do?" His voice soothed me. I wished he would just hold me and whisper softly to me. For a moment, I allowed myself to just soak up the temporary feeling of peace.

"I don't know. Maybe I can get some overtime at the Ration Center, work double shifts or something, but when would I see mom? Or you?"

Wes shrugged, clearly frustrated. "What if I put some of my savings towards the surgery?"

"Unless you have six grand, I don't know if it will help much."

He gave a low whistle. "Well…I have about two thousand."

A few tears fell onto my bare arms. "It's ok, Wes. I appreciate it, but I'll figure something out."

He gently grabbed my hands and looked at me. "Hey, stop trying to do everything by yourself. I *want* to give you the money."

I glanced up at him. The look in his eyes made my stomach flutter. His face stern, but full of love, sent a sudden, intense wave of desire through me. I couldn't pretend that I didn't think about the fact that we sat alone in my apartment, in my bedroom no less. I gently brushed a loose curl from his eye, feeling each nervous beat of my heart.

"I love you, Wes," I whispered. It just came out. I hadn't planned on telling him, I just thought it. A strange fear rose up within me, fear that I'd given myself to him, that I'd completely let down my walls and welcomed him in. But as I looked at him, I knew everything with him felt right. I *did* love him. And I wanted him to know.

A sudden grin broke over his face, followed by a look of both surprise and thrill. He gently brushed my cheek with his fingers. "I love you too, Lil." He took my hand in his and kissed it. "I've wanted to tell you, but I was afraid you'd think we were moving too fast."

"I don't." I smiled. "It's hard to believe I was such a jerk to you before."

"Yeah, I never thought we'd get to this point," he laughed. "But you were worth the abuse."

He laughed again as he dodged my punch. I leaned back against my pillows and held his hand. The money would help so much, but how could I take it from him?

"Thank you," I whispered.

"For what?"

"For offering your savings. You probably had them for a reason, and I hate to see you using them on me."

"I didn't really have them for anything, Lil. Maybe I started saving knowing they'd go to a good cause someday."

I smiled wanly and squeezed his hand. "It won't be enough, though, and I only have about five hundred saved from working so far."

"We'll figure something out." He reached down and gave me a hug. "In the meantime, I'm really tired. Can I crash on your couch tonight?"

"Yeah, let me get you some blankets," I offered. My arms and legs felt stiff and groggy, and it took me a minute to realize why. I still wore my clothes from earlier. I quickly slipped into some shorts and a tank top, then grabbed a spare blanket from the linen closet. He stood by the couch, staring down at a picture of me on the end table. I stood for a moment, taking him in, kicking myself for all the times I'd been so cruel to him.

"Sorry." He'd looked up and noticed me. "I just couldn't help looking at your picture. It's beautiful."

"Thanks," I replied. Suddenly the room felt too hot. I felt an unbearable longing to feel his hot skin under my hands, his protective arms wrapped around me in a warm embrace. He came closer, gently pulled me towards him and kissed he softly.

"Goodnight, my love," he whispered. A thick fog settled in my brain, keeping me from answering. How could he be so calm? My heart practically pounded out of my chest. I whispered a hurried goodnight and slipped back into my room, trying hard to slow my racing heart.

Finally, I climbed into bed. I tried to stay awake and calculate how I would get the other four thousand dollars, but thoughts only wandered back to Wes until my eyelids drooped.

Something felt strange, off-kilter. Instead of the warmth of my covers, I found myself drowning in cool darkness. I opened my eyes and looked around. Dark trees shrouded in mist surrounded me.

I'm dreaming.

Something felt wrong about this forest. But what?

I took a few tentative steps. Rustling sounded all around me. Fear clutched my heart, heightening my senses, tensing my muscles.

A low growl rose behind me, peaking my terror until I felt paralyzed. As I slowly turned around, I saw what terrified me most. A tall, emaciated man stood facing me. Eerie, flashing eyes.

A yellowy scalp, completely devoid of hair. Teeth, fingernails, grown beyond normal length. A beast.

My scream didn't stop, didn't diminish, only got louder and louder. The beast shot forward, grabbed me with his rough claws, shook me. I struggled, fought against the grip, but he held on, his hands strong and unclenching...

"Lily!"

I opened my eyes and gasped. Wes held me by the shoulders, a look of alarm on his face. "What happened?"

"The dream, it was so real..."

"It was just a dream, Lil. Don't worry about it."

I clutched him, my heart thudding at a frantic pace. How could I tell him what I'd seen? How could I explain that somehow I knew that something bad would happen soon, something that involved the beasts?

Chapter Nineteen

I tried to push down the feeling of nausea. It had been so real, the look of the beast's eyes, his claws digging into my skin. I shivered a little, despite the shafts of light from the rising sun streaming in through my window. I guessed it was around seven or so. In an hour and a half, I'd be in the Mainframe. The thought made my throat dry.

"Maybe it's just stress, Lil," he said.

"Maybe…"

For some reason, I couldn't bring myself to tell him about the dream. I shook it off, trying to focus on the warm sunshine, the fact that Wes sat here with me, but the fear still lingered. Everything had been so real, so vivid…

I pushed down the waves of terror washing over me. "I have to get ready for the Summons."

He drummed his fingers nervously on my bedspread. "I think you should ignore it."

I stared at him. "Did you not read the letter? Including the part about severe penalty if I don't go?"

"I'm really scared, Lil. What if it's a trap? What if you never come out?"

I rolled my eyes. "Don't be such a drama queen…er, king or whatever. I'll be fine."

Then, in a lightning bolt of inspiration it came to me. The answer I needed became so clear, so obvious that it made me feel stupid for not having thought of it before. I gasped, making Wes jump a little. "I know how to pay for mom's surgery!"

I jumped out of bed and rushed around, getting ready. The plan formed perfectly in my head. It would work…it had to work. If it didn't work, no other plan would.

"What do you mean?" Wes stood up, his face drawn in a frown.

"The Mainframe! They're *loaded*, and they want me bad, right?"

"Right…" His frown deepened. "So what?"

"So if they really want me, they'll give me an advance on my pay in the military. I can use that to get mom her surgery in Ithaca and I'll come back and join up after she's recovering!"

"Whoa, whoa, hang on," Wes interrupted. He took my hands in his. "First of all, how do we know you'll even get the advance, and second of all, do you know what it would mean to join up? Why do you think my mom and I have done *everything* we can to keep me out of the war? It's a slaughter, Lily. They're man-hunting the people of Epirus, thinking that if we kill enough of them we can invade!"

I stepped back, repulsed, then tried to shake it off. Mom's more important than anything, and I'd do what I needed to keep her alive. Even if it meant joining up.

"How do you even know that?" I raised my eyebrows skeptically.

"The Underground, Lily! Even some of the big-wigs at the D.o.D. are saying that's what it's like down there. And with your...abilities, who knows what they'll do to you. If you have some kind of super DNA, they'll be testing you and maybe even kill you to get what they want."

Fear and determination fought fiercely in my mind. Wes did work at the Defense Department and could be right, but mom would die in two months if I didn't do something. How else could I save her?

"I have to, Wes. I can't let her die. What if it was your mom?"

He opened his mouth, then paused. I'd struck a chord.

"You understand, don't you?"

He nodded mutely. "But I don't want to lose you, Lil."

"I'm tough. I can take care of myself." I smiled bravely, but his eyes dropped to the floor and his shoulders sagged. It broke my heart, but I put on a mask of forced cheerfulness. Wes had been so strong for me all this time. It was the least I could do for him now.

Half an hour later, we pulled into his employee parking spot. I gently took his hand and squeezed it. "Thanks for coming with me."

"No prob." He stared down at my hand in his.

"It isn't the end, you know. If Victor agrees, I'll have time with mom before I'm drafted. Maybe I can figure out a way to get out of it."

"If he's giving you a couple grand, he'll make sure there's no way you can get out of it."

I felt my face drop with disappointment. *He's right,* I reasoned, *but it's all I can do for her.*

He moved to get out of the car, but I grabbed his arm.

"What?" he asked.

"Just remember…don't stop me in there. You have to let me do this."

He frowned uneasily. "Lily…"

"Promise me, Wes."

He sighed. "I promise."

We walked across the lot to the sliding glass doors on the front of the building. The reception room of the Mainframe blew me away the instant we stepped in. The whole room, walls, floor, pillars, were made of pure marble. The ceilings towered over us, with large windows letting in light at the top. Longer windows lined the walls between the pillars, and the glass seemed to glitter. The idea of so much extravagance when people starved on the streets just blocks away sickened me.

We walked up to a bored, dirty-blonde secretary. Wes flashed his ID badge and the girl waved him back.

"Why do they even stay open on Saturdays if no one is here?"

Wes shrugged. "Some people work seven days a week, depending on which faction of the Mainframe they're in. The secretaries have to be here for them."

We stepped into a glass elevator that took us up to what felt like the top floor. As we stepped out, we faced another set of glass doors with the words "Head of Defense: Victor Channing" stamped on them. Wes stepped up to a retinal and fingerprint scanner. Once the machine verified his credentials, the doors clicked open. It suddenly struck me how much harder it would've been to come here without him. I felt a rush of gratitude and regret. I had Wes with me now, but for how long? What would Victor dictate?

"Does he work on Saturdays?" I asked, trying to distract myself from my thoughts.

"Yeah," Wes replied. "I guess he's always at work. Practically lives here."

I followed him to a huge mahogany reception desk. More extravagance. The dark-haired secretary looked up.

"Can I help you?" she asked in clipped tones.

"We're here to see Vic," Wes replied.

"He's not taking appointments today."

"I'm scheduled to see him today." She shrugged. "I'm Lily Mitchell."

The secretary looked up sharply. I held out the slightly-crumpled letter and she took it in her red-taloned fingers. Her eyes flew across the paper, taking in the contents over and over again.

"Everything seems to be in order." Without looking up, she pushed a small green button on an intercom. "What is it, Yvette? I'm busy," came a voice over the tiny speaker. I recognized the oily voice.

"You have a Lily Mitchell here."

A door down a back hall suddenly burst open. Victor Channing came strutting down the hallway. He looked much shorter than he did on TV.

"We've been expecting you, Miss Mitchell. Please come back to my office. Your escort will not need to follow." I shrank back slightly at the almost-hungry look on his face.

"Sorry, but I won't go in without him." I clenched my fists to keep my hands still.

He rubbed his chin thoughtfully, then a creepy smile suddenly spread across his face. "Of course, Miss Mitchell. Right this way."

I looked at Wes uneasily. He shrugged. Not really knowing what else to do, I followed the creepy slimeball to an office the size of my whole apartment. A gigantic television screen covered one wall with several different memos floating across the screen, some about wanted criminals, some with maps of the city and others with lists of instructions. The opposite wall held huge windows that looked out over the city. I saw my apartment complex in the distance, rising like a brown hunchback among all the shabby gray buildings of the slums. Victor sat down in a fancy leather chair behind his desk and poured himself a large measure of whiskey.

"Care for some?" he asked, holding up the bottle. I shook my head in disgust. Wes didn't bother with a reply. He shrugged and leaned back in his chair.

"So…I'm sure you know why we've summoned you."

"Your drones told me I'd join up one way or another."

"Ah, well, it's wonderful to see that you're cooperating so nicely. Your…special talents would be most useful to us."

He didn't offer a chair, so I sat down in a hard, uncomfortable one in front of his desk. Wes took the other spare chair.

"I'm not just coming here to offer myself. I have one condition that has to be met before I do anything."

Wes looked like he wanted to say something, but I silenced him with a warning look. He clenched his fists, clearly fighting the urge to punch Victor. At least that's what I figured because I felt like punching the slimeball too. Yet underneath my anger and contempt for this man, I felt a strangely familiar undercurrent of fear. Terror gripped my heart as I recognized the feeling as the same one I'd gotten around the beasts. But how could that be possible? Surely the Head of Defense wasn't a beast. I studied him carefully, but he looked nothing like the beasts I'd seen.

"Really?" Victor laughed softly. "You think you can negotiate with us?"

"Do it or you don't have me. When I walk out of this office, I'll disappear."

He laughed again, making me hate him even more. "Where to, miss? You don't have anywhere to go. Your mother is your only family. And the poor dear has cancer. I don't think you'd do something so heartless as leaving her."

I felt a ripple of panic and pushed it down. "Yeah, I know your creeps have been trailing me, but I'll get away. I have a plan, and if you don't listen to me, you won't have me for your stupid war." Ok, it wasn't true, I had no plan, but I'd figure something out. Hopefully.

He sat up a little, the satisfied smirk still plastered all over his face. "Ok, then, let's hear your conditions."

I took a deep breath, willing myself to calm down. "Pay for my mom to receive the Barbach treatment. As soon as she's cleared by her doctors and on the mend, I'll report for duty."

"No." Wes said it quietly. I shot him a glance again. His lips turned white, contrasting sharply against his red face. "You can't."

I shrugged slightly. "I'm sorry," I whispered.

"Do you have any idea how much that costs, missy?" Victor's voice, no longer oily but icy sharp, cut through my thoughts.

"Yes, I do. And don't call me missy."

"It's a lot of cash to spend on something that's not defense-related." He laughed again, condescendingly. "You're such a teenager, thinking the world owes you everything."

I stood up, seething, trying not to lose control. "You *will* do it, or I'm not working for you! I know what I am, and I know I'm your only hope for building your stupid super-army. Do NOT underestimate me!"

For a split second, something like alarm flashed across his face. I wondered if I really looked that intimidating. But as quickly as the fearful look appeared, it vanished. He sat up.

"Is that a threat?"

"I'll let you decide," I hissed. "Are you going to give me what I want or not?"

He paused, twirling his finger around the top of his glass. "How do I know you'll come back?"

"Keep in touch with the hospital. Dr. Andrew Dennison will keep you informed of my mom's progress. The minute you hear she's out of the hospital and settled, you'll know I'm coming."

He regarded me again, that creepy gleam in his eye. "You're serious, aren't you?"

"Dead serious."

He stood up and went to a wall safe. After punching in a series of complicated numbers, the safe swung open. He pulled out a device about the same size as the datacard in my communicator.

"Well, you asked for it," he said. "We use this for our soldiers to ensure they do not go AWOL. It's a tracking device that attaches to your neck, you barely notice it."

"How does it work?" I asked cautiously.

"It has microscopic clamps that attach to your skin. It feels like a slight pinprick."

I swallowed hard. Wes called it. Victor made sure I couldn't slip through the cracks. I stared at the tiny, menacing tracker. My life would end when I put it on, but mom's life depended on it.

"What about my mom's treatment? How do I know you'll keep up your end of the deal?"

"I'll transfer the funds to your communicator right now if you like. You can see it clear as day and pay for the treatment as soon as you leave."

I handed him my communicator. "Do it."

"Let me put the device on you first," he said. "It'll only take a minute."

"No, you put the funds on first."

He laughed again. "Do you really think I'm that stupid, Miss Mitchell?"

I narrowed my eyes. "You can figure that one out for yourself. I'll let you put your dumb thing on me, but transfer the funds so I can see you doing it. Then you can hold my communicator while you put that thing on me. And I swear, if you try to pull anything with me, I'll smash your nose into your brain."

For a moment, I scared myself. I wasn't sure where the threat came from. I didn't usually threaten strangers, but I shrugged it off. Desperate times, desperate measures, as people used to say. Uneasiness flashed across his face for a moment.

"Fine," he replied decisively.

He took my communicator and held it out for me to see. "What do you need?"

I looked at Wes. He shrugged, his lips still drawn tight in fury. "I have enough for travel expense on the speed train, and two thousand dollars. I need about four thousand more."

With a few quick taps, he transferred the money to the tiny amount in my account.

I couldn't believe my good luck. He didn't even try to shortchange me. It struck me suddenly that they really needed me. They were *desperate* for me. The thought made my head spin. How could I be that valuable?

A sudden elation filled my whole body. Mom would live. She'd stay with me for years to come. The treatment would work as it had on so many others. Tears of joy crept into my eyes.

The elation wore off, however, when Victor stepped behind me, my communicator in one hand and the tracking chip in the other, reminding me that I'd just sold myself to the Mainframe. I thought about struggling, slipping away, but who knew what this Victor guy could do? He might shoot me right there in his office. Reluctantly, I closed my eyes and felt a slight prick on my neck, followed by a light electrical tingle.

"The shock you felt means that the tracking device has read and made a blueprint of your DNA. It's uniquely yours now. Also, the device injects a small amount of paralysis drug into you if you remove it. It's not a lethal amount, but enough to paralyze you until we find you."

My heart sank as I nodded quietly. What had I gotten myself into? I looked at Wes, who stood staring at the floor, his fists clenched at his sides.

"We'll be in touch with the hospital. Once your mother has been moved from the hospital permanently, I will be in touch again." Victor handed me my communicator and I looked at the account information one more time just to make sure. With my savings, I had just over forty-five thousand. With Wes's money, it would be enough.

Relief, fear, fatigue, anger and regret washed through me all at the same time, but I hid it under a brisk nod to Victor. I didn't want him to see how truly afraid I felt.

"We'll see you soon, Lily."

His last words haunted me all the way down the hall, down the elevator and out into the parking lot.

Chapter Twenty

We left the building and got into Wes's car, neither of us speaking. The awful truth sank into me like a shot at the doctor. The Mainframe owned me. The tracker tugged at my skin uncomfortably.

"I'm sorry," I croaked. He looked at me, his eyes red. I pulled him into a hug, wrapping my arms tightly around him. I kissed him fiercely, feeling the surprise in his lips. As we pulled apart, he leaned his forehead against mine.

"I know why you did it, Lil, and I understand. But…I'll miss you terribly. I don't think I'll ever stop worrying about you."

At that, I lost control completely. I sobbed on his shoulder for what felt like the hundredth time since we first kissed.

"I'll find a way to get out of it," I choked. "Somehow."

He stroked my cheek with his fingers. "I'll help you. I won't let you go."

I nodded slowly and suddenly remembered mom. We needed to get to the hospital and pay for the treatment. "We've got to go."

He nodded back and revved the engine. He stayed silent, avoiding my eyes the whole drive to the hospital. I tried to tell him again how sorry I felt, how I regretted now what I'd done, but he got out of the car the second we pulled into the parking lot. Hope struggled to rise through my gloom as we walked into the hospital and found Dr. Dennison.

"Lily, I was wondering when you'd be back," he said. "Are you all right?"

It took me a minute to remember my spell from the night before. So much happened since then…

"I'm fine," I lied, hoping my eyes weren't still red and puffy. "I…have the money. For the treatment."

His eyebrows shot up towards his receding gray hairline. "You *do*? How?"

I looked at Wes. "It's a long story," I replied, feeling the bug on my neck prickle again.

Half an hour later, we sat with mom, telling her the news. She bounced back and forth between beaming and crying.

"Lily…what did you do to get the money?" she asked.

"Don't worry about it, mom." I spoke gently, trying to avoid the burning look from Wes. "All that matters is that you're going to get better."

When the doctor came in a short while later and busied her with paperwork, Wes looked at me grimly. "You're going to have to tell her at some point."

"I know." I blinked back tears. "I just couldn't do it yet. Not now that she's so happy."

He started to say something back, but the doctor turned to me. "Will you be accompanying your mother?"

"Yes," I replied. "I should have enough for two Speedrail tickets. When do we need to leave?"

"I've already spoken with the Ithaca surgeons and wired over her history on my communicator. They want your mom there by tomorrow given the progress of her condition. They'll start the operation in the morning."

He handed me a copy of itinerary, gave me some more paperwork to fill out, then connected me to the Speedrail main page on my communicator so that I could get tickets. As soon as the purchase went through, the tickets printed out of the little printer on the side, one reading Elaine Mitchell and the other reading Lily Mitchell. After that, I worked with the doctor to get the funds transferred to the hospital in Ithaca where the surgery would take place. I had a very small amount left for food and other incidentals.

I suddenly felt very overwhelmed. We'd have to leave by tonight, and that meant these were my last few hours with Wes. He still sat by the bed. He caught my eye and nodded understandingly.

As soon as the doctors left, I came close to mom and held her hand in mine. "Mom…do you mind if I go with Wes to get some clothes for us from home? We have to leave tonight if we're going to make it for your operation."

"That's fine, honey." She squeezed my hand and smiled.

"Good luck, Elaine," said Wes quietly. She smiled up at him.

"Thank you, Wes. We'll see you when we get home."

He smiled grimly and took my hand. As we left the room, I suddenly felt crippled by all the emotions raging through me. I couldn't leave Wes, but mom would live. Then again, who knew if I'd ever see her again after her surgery? How could such opposing feelings fly through me all at once? I felt the bug on my neck and longed again to rip it off and throw it over the cliffs into the ocean.

Wes and I drove back to my apartment in silence.

"I'm so sorry, Wes." It felt like the thousandth time I'd told him, but I couldn't help feeling horrible and wanting to apologize.

"For what? You did what you had to." His tone, defeated and limp, sent a pang of sadness through my heart.

"For dragging you into this. You've hardly had a life since we started dating." I hung my head and stared at my hands.

He took one of my hands and kissed it. "Lily, I wouldn't take back these weeks we've had together for anything."

He hugged me briefly before getting out of the car, trying to hide his face from me. I couldn't hold back my own tears as I slowly followed him up the stairs to my apartment. I tried to ignore my growing terror as I numbly gathered some clothes and a couple packages of food.

"Lily...do you want to go to the beach?" Wes asked suddenly.

I stared at him for a moment, taken aback. "What time is it?"

He pulled out his communicator and glanced at it. "Noon."

I'd bought tickets for the six o' clock train. We only had a few hours, but I couldn't say no.

"Yes."

Soon we drove down the highway to the beach. The sun loomed high in the sky, but thankfully people stayed away from the beach today. Wes helped me out of the car and took my hand. I stared out at the waves as we walked along the shore.

"Are you ok?" I asked him. He glanced at me with that smile of his.

"I will be," he replied. "As soon as I figure out how to get you out of this mess."

He stopped suddenly and turned towards me. I looked up into his hollow eyes. He leaned down slowly and brushed my lips with his.

"Lily, will you promise me something?" he whispered as we pulled apart.

I put my hands around his shoulders and pulled him closer. "What?"

He took a deep breath. "Promise me that you'll escape somehow, that we'll find each other no matter what happens."

I blinked back tears and traced his jaw with my fingers. "I already did."

"No, I mean really promise me. I don't know why, but I just have an odd feeling. Tell me that you'll find a way out, that you'll find me if something happens."

I stepped back, scared. He acted like he'd die as soon as I left, like he wanted me to find his body.

"Don't talk like that, Wes." My voice trembled. "We'll find each other, and things will work out. This war won't last forever."

"Please just promise me," he whispered, his eyes growing wide with urgency.

I grabbed his hands. "Ok. I promise."

He wrapped his arms around me and kissed me again, passionate, intense, both of us wanting so much more and hating the fact that we couldn't have it. His lips brushed my neck, my ears, my cheeks again and again. As we finally pulled apart, he pushed my hair gently back from my forehead.

"Let me know when you come back from Ithaca. I'll be waiting for you."

I held back my tears as wrapped my arms around his waist. "I'll try. I don't know what's going to happen."

He smiled wanly. "Don't worry, Lil. We'll find each other again."

I tried to smile, but I could see the same worry and fear that I felt reflected in his eyes. It seemed hopeless, pretending we might see each other again, but I couldn't let him see my doubt. With one last kiss, we walked slowly back to his car.

Chapter Twenty-One

The Speedrail moved silently across the darkening landscape. Mom lay next to me, asleep, completely worn out after being moved from the hospital to the special car of the train. Honestly, I liked it that way. I could barely see the passing hills for the tears in my eyes, and mom would only ask questions if she saw me.

Wes stayed in my heart, my thoughts the whole long ride to Ithaca. How could I have just given him up like that? The moment the train pulled away and I watched Wes wave goodbye, I felt like a part of me ripped away and stayed with him, leaving a huge, gaping hole in my heart.

I leaned my head against the cool glass, trying to ignore the constant ache, but it wouldn't go away. I still felt his lips on mine, his strong arms around me, his gentle fingers running through my hair.

Mom stirred in her sleep, so I tucked her blankets back around her. My body shimmered with sweat in the hot car, but she shivered slightly. I pulled my hair back from my sticky neck and felt the tracking bug still resting on my skin. A surge of fierce anger swept through me. I wanted to tear it off again and throw it out the window. Maybe it would throw them off for a few days while they tried to find my body.

I tried to concentrate on the rolling hills outside. I'd never really been outside the city except to go to the beach, and I'd certainly never seen country like this. Some of it rolling green hills, other parts of it covered in sage and sand. I knew the train moved farther inland, to a place that dry and cold instead of moist and warm like the coast.

We finally pulled into the large Ithaca station around nine. The ambulance for the Ithaca hospital stood there in the parking lot, waiting for us. Mom woke up and smiled at me until she noticed my red eyes.

"Missing Wes?"

I nodded and tried to smile. "It's ok. I'll be all right."

"Well, you'll see him when we get home, honey. Don't worry."

She smiled reassuringly and I tried to smile back, feeling my heart breaking all over again. If only she knew…

"Let's get you to the hospital," I said, trying to distract myself from my pain. The ambulance crew greeted us kindly and loaded mom into the back. I sat with her as the ambulance lumbered through the city. Through the windows, I saw glimpses of the city. The streets looked so clean and I couldn't see any tramps wandering around. Huge, glittering buildings lined the main boulevard, a stark contrast to the lumpy-looking black and gray buildings back home.

I couldn't stop myself from gasping as we got out of the ambulance at the hospital. The building looked like a castle, vastly different to the sterile, ugly, concrete building back home. Floors and floors of rooms towered above us.

The lobby looked a lot like the Mainframe building, with marble floors and shiny wooden desks. A sliding glass door stood in each of the hallways that branched off to different parts of the hospital. I followed the ambulance crew into a silver elevator that pinged when we finally reached the floor we needed. As we stepped out, I gasped again at the beauty and décor of the room. The same polished wooden desks stood by the elevator with the words "Cancer Unit" stamped into them in gold lettering.

"Mrs. Mitchell?" said the woman at the desk pleasantly. Ithaca confused me with its clean, sparkly beauty. People here were pleasant, happy…healthy. It felt so different from Arduba.

"Yes," said mom. It took her a while to answer. She stared around at the surroundings, completely astounded like me.

"Right this way."

The ambulance crew wheeled her through some more sliding glass doors to a comfortable room. The chairs weren't the ugly pink plastic variety like Arduba's hospital. They were actually cushioned, with padding that didn't look a hundred years old. Live ferns adorned the corners of the room, and sliding glass doors across the way led to an actual balcony with a pristine granite railing, unlike the cheap metal railing that enclosed our apartment complex stairs. A huge bed lay next to a comfortable cot, both made up with smooth, satiny sheets.

"We'll let you get settled," said one of the nurses who accompanied us. "The doctor will be in soon to discuss the treatment plan and set you up for tomorrow."

The ambulance crew helped mom onto the bed and settled in the silky sheets. The crew left and I perched on the cot next to her bed.

Mom smiled. "Can you believe this? I've never seen anything like this!"

I grinned back. "It's incredible. I wonder if the rest of the country is like this or the capitol."

Mom shrugged. "Well, do you want…"

She was cut off by the arrival of the doctor and surgeon, a tall, good-looking man in his early thirties.

"Ah, Mrs. Mitchell and your daughter Lily, we've been expecting you. Andrew told me all about you and we're excited to meet you. I'm Tony Thatcher, your doctor."

"Thank you," said mom, blushing as he shook her hand. He flashed a brilliant smile at her and looked down at his chart.

"The procedure will take about four hours and you'll need to rest for twenty-four hours after that. Then we'll inject the rest of the healing serum after the twenty-four hour period. We'll ask you to stay one more day just to make sure everything is going as planned. As soon as your tests clear, you can go home! Pretty simple, huh?"

Mom smiled again, a bright smile that I hadn't seen in a long time. "Sounds wonderful," she replied. I felt a rush of relief tainted by the realization that we'd be in Ithaca three days at the most. Vic probably knew by now how long the procedure would take. In my mind, he had become a hunter, just waiting for me to wander back into range before he could trap me. The thought made me sick.

"Lily, I know you'll want to stay here with your mom, but you're welcome to leave the hospital and explore while she's under. Or you can stay here. Our physical therapy pool on the bottom floor is open when appointments are not in session, you have a television in your room and we have a full service cafeteria on the third floor. It's up to you."

"Thanks," I replied with another attempt at a smile. "I think I just want to go to sleep."

I hadn't realized until just then how tired I felt. Mom looked pretty sleepy too. Dr. Thatcher talked about a few more minor preparatory procedures that mom would undergo, then left. Shortly after, the cafeteria brought up a meal unlike any I'd ever seen in Arduba's hospital cafeteria. Instead of the bland processed meat ration and freeze-dried vegetables, the plate held a real steak, a steamy baked potato smothered in real butter and cream and *bread*. Real, wheat bread covered in a layer of the same delicious-looking butter. Real wheat had become so expensive, almost impossible to grow, but there it sat. The food tasted more delicious than anything I'd ever eaten. Mom and I ate like pigs, not bothering to wonder how they had gotten their hands on real meat, bread and potatoes.

With a full stomach and a comfy bed, I soon fell asleep. I didn't wake up until I felt the sun on my face streaming in from the window. I couldn't figure out why I felt so awful and so wonderful at the same time until I felt the tracker bug again on my neck. I looked over at mom, sleeping peacefully. My heart sank as I wondered if the Mainframe would even let me say goodbye to her when we got home.

A short while later, a large team of nurses and doctors came in and got mom ready to go into surgery. Dr. Thatcher patted my back and smiled.

"You've had a rough couple months, haven't you?" he asked, his blue eyes twinkling.

I nodded, not really knowing what to say. He squeezed my arm reassuringly. "Well, she'll be right as rain soon. The Barbach Treatment hasn't failed yet."

I should have been ecstatic, but his words didn't cheer me up. I'd gotten my mom a cure just to say goodbye to her, maybe forever. I mustered up a smile and slipped away to see mom.

"This is all thanks to you, Lily," she whispered with a smile. "I love you, honey."

"I love you too, mom." I held her hand to my cheek and kissed it before they wheeled her away. Silence settled over the room as the busy team left, making everything suddenly gloomy. I stepped out on the balcony for a while and looked out over the city. People just started to move around. Newsstands and shops opened for the day. People greeted each other as they passed. It seemed like something out of a fairy tale.

I walked back into the cool room and looked for my suitcase. I riffled through the contents for some shorts and a tank top, but to my surprise, I found my red bikini lying in among my things. I must have grabbed it with a bunch of clothes since I'd been in such a hurry. I'd worn this one the day Wes and I surfed together on his board. I closed my eyes a moment, trying to recapture moments from that day, but they slipped through the cracks of my mind like sand through my fingers. That day felt like a hundred years ago instead of just a few weeks. I plodded down the hall to the elevator, thoroughly depressed.

The pool stretched across the large room, with a diving board and several handholds along the concrete edge, probably for the handicapped people who used these pools to regain movement. No one swam in the pool, thankfully, so I slipped into the pleasantly warm water. As I swam underwater and did a couple surface strokes, I tried to imagine being back at the beach with Wes, surfing and swimming in the cold salty water, but the warm, chlorinated water just didn't compare.

A couple hours later, I stepped out and dried off with one of the towels sitting in a small cart. My mind wandered to Wes as I sat by the side of the pool, and tears began to well up in my eyes. I had to keep busy, to keep myself from thinking of him.

An older woman in a bathing suit, followed by a younger man in trunks, came walking into the room. He wore a blue ID tag, same as the other doctors in the hospital, and I figured he'd come for his first appointment of the day. I excused myself and headed back up the elevator to my room.

I washed the chlorine out of my hair in the large shower adjoining mom's room. I'd never lived in such luxury in all my life. A nurse stocked the bathroom with scented soaps, shampoos and conditioners, not to mention little complimentary bottles of perfume. I took my time, washing every inch of my aching body in steaming hot water. Most people didn't have warm water for showers in the city, especially the lower income areas.

I finally stepped out and dried off with a warm fluffy towel, then wrapped it around my wet hair. I grabbed some comfortable jeans and an old t-shirt. Not knowing what else to do, I sat down on my cot and flipped the TV on and flipped over to the news.

"...state of emergency at the Department of Defense..."

I sat up at the newscaster's announcement and turned up the volume.

"Earlier this morning, a raid on the Department of Defense left some wounded but none killed. The guerillas swarmed the building, let in by some of the employees who turned traitor. Since the raid took place on Sunday morning, most Defense Personnel weren't notified quickly enough to stop the guerillas from stealing several valuable weapons from the Mainframe arsenals."

My heart froze. I knew Wes didn't work weekends, but what if he'd been involved in the attack somehow?

I glanced at my communicator lying on mom's bed where I'd left it. I knew it would be incredibly risky, but I had to try and get in touch with Wes.

I turned on voice command. "What name, please?" said the flat female voice.

"Wes Landon," I said hurriedly, making it sound more like Wesandn.

"Wayne Larson," she replied pleasantly. "One moment please."

"No, Wes Landon!" I screeched.

"I'm sorry. Wes Landon. Is that correct?"

"Yes. Please dial."

"Video or audio?"

"Video."

Within moments, the communicator connected to Wes. The video popped up, but I only saw blackness. I thought I heard a faint whisper, but I couldn't quite make it out.

"Wes?"

"Shhh!"

A faint light began to glow and I finally saw Wes's face. "Wes? Are you ok?"

"I can't talk, Lily," he whispered urgently. "I'm sorry."

"Why?" I whispered back.

"I'm in hiding. The raid caused an immediate draft. They're looking for me."

Chapter Twenty-Two

The screen suddenly went blank. Panic seized my heart, squeezing it like a fist, making it pump unnaturally fast.

"Wes? Wes!"

A stream of thoughts flew through my mind. I wanted to run to the train, get on right now and find him, but mom wouldn't be out of surgery for a while. I wanted to call him again, but the communicator lines were probably being watched. *I'm trapped,* I thought helplessly. Trapped like a wild beast in a small cage. Had they found him? Where had he hidden? What happened to him?

Abandoning reason, I tried dialing through again, but his number popped up unavailable. He must have taken himself off the network. Beads of sweat broke out on my forehead. I couldn't wait two whole days before mom could leave. Wes could be detained by then, or…

I wouldn't allow myself to think it. We'd made a promise that we'd be together. I knew Wes would keep his promise.

Not knowing what else to do, I glanced at the clock. Mom would be out of surgery any minute. Maybe the doctor would let her move sooner…

As if in answer to my thoughts, the doctor came in. "Your mom is all done, Lily. She pulled through just fine and is in the recovery unit right now."

I smiled despite my worry over Wes. "She's really going to be ok?"

"Yep. She'll be under for the next twenty-four hours in order to speed her healing, but should be up by tomorrow morning. She doesn't even have to go back into surgery for the serum. We'll just inject it in one of the smaller offices downstairs."

"Thanks for everything, doctor," I said.

"I'm glad we could help." He gave that broad smile of dazzling white teeth again and waved as he stepped out the door.

"Wait!" I called. He stepped back in and stuck a pen behind his ear. "Does she still need to stay all day tomorrow?"

He shrugged. "She did really well in surgery, but we'll have to see how she reacts to the serum."

"Ok."

He winked and stepped out into the hall again. A full-blown battle raged in my brain. On one hand, I wanted to delay going back home because of the promise I'd made to Vic. He would most likely only let me have one day with mom to get her comfortable. But on the other hand, I could use that day to search for Wes, wherever he hid, and maybe talk to his mom. But it all depended on how fast mom could heal. I clenched my fists in frustration. Either way, I couldn't win.

Half an hour later, mom came back. They brought her in on a gurney and transferred her to the bed. She didn't move a muscle. She definitely wouldn't wake up anytime soon. A team of nurses came in a while later and hooked her up to an IV so she would be fed while she slept. My own stomach rumbled, so I wandered aimlessly down to the cafeteria. The TV blared over the noise of the small crowd, so I grabbed a sandwich and sat down to watch. The newscaster just talked about the weather, but suddenly the camera switched to the main desk.

"And now, our top story from the capitol-Victor Channing, head of the Department of Defense, still has no news concerning the massive weapons raid earlier this morning, but believes the insurgents to be from the Southern Province. The Call to Arms is still in effect."

A list popped up in front of the blonde newscaster with several names. "If you or someone you know is on this list, it is imperative to report immediately to the Defense Department of the Mainframe for the Draft. Any persons who do not report by ten o'clock am tomorrow will be brought in by a Special Forces Team."

I scanned the list quickly to the L's and found his name. He managed to stay in hiding after all. Even though I'd never been particularly religious, I prayed fervently that he would be all right. I felt another pang of fear at the mention of the Special Forces Team. I had no idea what they were supposed to do, but it didn't sound good. And even if mom could leave tomorrow morning, it wouldn't make any difference. The Special Forces Team would be out tomorrow, looking for people avoiding the draft. I wished desperately that I wasn't three hours away and could help Wes. I could always take my return ticket to the station and exchange for a different time. So many Speedtrains left from a given station at once that it probably wouldn't be a problem. The thought tempted me so badly I could hardly bear it, but I couldn't leave mom to try and get home on her own.

I took a deep breath and tried to think of something, but trying to come up with an idea felt like running around in a maze. Dead end after dead end.

I finished my sandwich and took the elevator back up to mom's room. She still slept peacefully. I wondered vaguely why she had to sleep a whole twenty-four hours. The surgery must have been taxing.

The day passed agonizingly slowly, broken up only by visits from different nurses to check mom's healing progress on the monitors. The rest of the time, I checked the news, but the news crew only ran the same weather report or the Call to Arms.

Later, as I ate dinner, the Dr. Thatcher came in and looked at mom's vitals, then typed a bunch of stuff into his dataclip.

"She's really coming along, Lily. I don't think we have anything to worry about. She'll most likely react very well to the serum."

I nodded, lost in thought. I picked absently at a loose thread on my sleeve until he left. I didn't want to talk, even about mom's progress. It only mattered that the treatment had worked, that she'd stay alive. He took the hint and left after he finished with his information.

Suddenly, a strange booping noise came from my communicator. I sat up, immediately alert. It never made that sound before. The screen showed an incoming video call, but on a channel I didn't recognize. Timidly, I tapped the screen. A vaguely familiar woman's face popped up. I squinted at the screen for a long time before it hit me.

"Mrs. Landon," I whispered. "What's going on? I talked to Wes this morning, but it cut off-"

Her eyes darted nervously back and forth nervously. She didn't appear to be in a room, either. It looked like some kind of dark tunnel, with just the tiniest sliver of light playing across her face.

"I don't have much time to explain," she whispered urgently. "I'm on an illegal frequency, but I knew it was the only way to reach you. We're being watched."

"What's going on?" My heart hammered so loudly in my chest I felt sure she could hear it.

"Wes is on the run. He's going north, where his grandmother lives. We figure she's far enough away that it'll take them a while to find him. He'll stay a few days, then move on. He made me swear to tell you where he went, something about a promise..."

She babbled nervously, but for the first time in days I felt a warm surge of hope. Wes remembered our promise, and he'd escaped.

"But when will he be back?"

"He can't come back. When they don't find him tomorrow, he'll be considered a criminal. If they do find him, they might put him in jail to wait trial, but they'll most likely just ship him off to war."

Panicked tears began to trickle down my face. "No...no, he has to come back, he has to!"

She started to cry too. "He can't. I'm so sorry. I know he loves you very much, but it would be suicide to stay."

"But can you at least tell me what part of the country he'll be in? Please!"

"I have to go!" Her eyes grew wide with fear, sending a pang of terror through my heart.

"No, please! Tell me where I can find him, please!"

The screen flickered off and returned to a normal channel as if there'd been no interruption at all. I stared at the screen, tears streaming freely. Just like that, Wes was gone.

Chapter Twenty-Three

I woke up cramped and stiff the next day, having fallen asleep in my chair with my communicator clutched in my hands. My eyes felt sore and puffy since I'd cried until I had no more tears. The doctor already stood next to mom's bed, working with a team to move her into a wheelchair. She looked so healthy and happy, but worried.

Luckily, she waited until we sat in a small office on one of the lower floors to ask me what happened. I looked at her, trying to decide where to begin.

"Can we wait until we're back in the room, mom?"

She hesitated. "Ok…but I'm worried. You look like you didn't sleep very well."

I shrugged and attempted a smile. "I'm ok. Glad that you're better. Dr. Thatcher said the surgery went really well."

"I feel so different. It's like I've been scrubbed clean on the inside. I don't feel any pain anymore." She smiled and looked suddenly ten years younger. My heart struggled to feel light under the heavy burden it carried. I felt ecstatic about mom, but completely heartbroken over Wes. Once again, I wondered how two such conflicting emotions could exist together.

Dr. Thatcher came in soon after and gave mom a few shots of serum. He checked the site of the shot, then checked her vitals. Mom stayed alert the entire time.

"How do you feel, Elaine?" he asked, frowning in concentration as he stared at his dataclip.

"Great!" she exclaimed.

"Well, you seem stable enough. You did great in the surgery, but I think I'd like you to stay an extra day just to get your strength up before the long trip."

My heart sank slightly, but I couldn't do anything anyway. Wes had probably found his grandmother by now. Mom, however, beamed at the words, obviously thrilled to stay in lush comfort for another day. I smiled as best I could, dreading the conversation that would follow when we went back upstairs.

The doctor and some nurses helped mom hobble over to her wheelchair. He explained some of her charts and vitals, but I only half listened. After a few nods and smiles, I took mom to the elevator. The upstairs nurse helped her into bed.

"Now are you going to tell me what's going on?" She fixed me with her penetrating stare and I looked quickly down at my hands. Where to begin?

"Wes…is gone." The words sounded like an echo, as if I listened to someone else.

She frowned. "What do you mean?"

I closed my eyes and took a deep breath. "He had to escape." I told her the entire situation, starting with the break-in at the Mainframe and Wes's sudden run to freedom. Her face went sheet white when I explained how I'd gotten the treatment paid for.

"Lily, they'll take you as soon as you get to the city! You can't go back!"

"They've got a tracker on me, mom. I can't escape." I lifted my hair and showed her the small disc attached to my neck. "Besides, you know I wouldn't desert you."

Mom frowned deeply. "Well…what if someone else wore your tracker?"

I shook my head fiercely. "Mom, I know what you're thinking and the answer is no. Who knows what they'd do to you if they found you and not me. Besides, it's created to inject a paralyzing drug if I try to take it off. I'd be stuck anyway."

"What if you told them it came off? You could claim that you were scratching your neck or something and it just slipped off. Since you're out of town, they'd know you need to wait until you get back."

"Yeah, but I'd still be paralyzed," I argued.

"I'm sure Dr. Thatcher knows what kind of drug they put in there and has an antidote or something. You could tell the Mainframe that the hospital took care of it and that you'll keep your bug with you."

I laughed hollowly. "Like they'll believe that."

"They're not as perfect as they act, Lily. Everyone makes mistakes. It's worth a shot."

"What would I do then? I don't have anywhere to go but back to the city."

She paused for a moment, thinking. "What if you found Wes?"

I stared at her unbelievingly. "You want me to leave you to go find Wes? I can't, mom. I can't send you back to the city alone and flit off into oblivion."

"What if I stayed here?" she countered.

"The hospital won't pay for you to stay, mom, they have other patients."

She smiled slyly. "I never told you that I had an old high school friend that moved up here, did I? For all I know, she might still be here."

"Yeah, but she's probably married and changed her name. Would she even remember you?"

"Would you quit arguing? She did get married about ten years ago and I got an invitation. If she remembered me then, she should remember me now." She shook her head at me and gently took my hands in hers. "I know you're in love with Wes, Lily. If it were me and your dad, I…I wouldn't give up until I found him."

A look of deep sadness flashed across her face for a moment, making her look haggard again for just a moment. I felt a strange twinge in my heart. She loved my dad, she'd had a child with him. I loved Wes, but we'd just started dating. Could I really plunge off into the unknown after him?

But then I thought of his gentle eyes, the way he'd taken me home after my collapse in the hospital. I thought of the way he'd looked at my picture that night in the apartment. He loved me, and I had fallen completely in love with him.

Mom cleared her throat and took out her communicator. She started looking through the database of information.

"Aha! There are three Annie Johnsons listed within the city limits." A smug smile crossed her face. "See? Now all I have to do is call them."

Mom opted for the audio option on each call, and actually got lucky on the second. She talked enthusiastically with this friend I never even knew existed.

"Wait, let me switch to video," said the high-pitched, ultra-feminine voice on the line. "Elaine, I can't believe it's really you! You look wonderful!"

"You too, Annie. It's so good to see you!"

"When are you coming to visit me? It's been way too long since we caught up."

"Actually, I'm in your neck of the woods right now," mom laughed. "And I have a huge favor to ask you."

She explained the situation, but made it sound like she wanted to stay in Ithaca for her health, saying that the country air would do her good.

"What about Lily?"

Mom carefully avoided glancing in my direction. "She's with me now, but she has to be back to work in the city in a couple days. All the pollution in the city is a bit much, and the doctor said it would be better if I could stay where the air is more breathable."

Annie readily agreed, opting to let mom stay in her guest bedroom. "When will you be released?"

"Probably tomorrow morning," mom replied. "Are you sure this is ok?"

"Oh, absolutely," she laughed. "It'll be just like old times!"

Mom laughed along and chatted a while longer with Annie. They made arrangements for Annie to pick mom up at the hospital the following day, then said goodbye. I stared at mom, realizing just how little I knew about her past. She usually didn't want to talk about her childhood. She turned to me, unexpectedly brisk and businesslike.

"Now we need to get that bug off of you."

My hand went automatically to the tracker. "Yeah, but mom...I still don't have a plan. They're expecting me to come back with my tracker."

"Yes, but you haven't listened to my idea yet. Go to the train station tomorrow morning like they expect you to. Get on the train to Illyria, drop the tracker and then get off, pretending like you got the wrong train. Then get on a northern train. They'll trace you to the train, but won't know what to do when you're not on it."

"Yeah, but mom I have no idea where he went. He could be as far north as Parthin. And where would I stay?" Since when did she become so reckless?

"Well, do some research of your own. You said Wes would stay at his grandmother's a few days, so start with his last name and see if there are any people with that last name living in any of the major cities up north."

I shrugged, feeling odd. I knew mom would be safe here, but I still felt scared to leave her alone. And besides, we probably wouldn't be able to communicate once I left. Mom took extra care on her communicator to make it sound like I would go back to the city because they might have been listening.

I browsed the information for the city of Parthin, but couldn't find any Landons. I tried Dorsi, a town a little further south, next. No luck.

"Mom, this is hopeless. I've tried a couple towns, but there aren't any Landons. It's probably his mom's grandparents anyway. His dad seemed like kind of a deadbeat."

"Do you know her maiden name at all?"

"No." I stared out the window. All the hope that inadvertently grew inside me while mom talked to Annie started to shrink into nothing.

"What about finding their marriage certificate?"

I rolled my eyes. "Like they'd just release that on the database."

Mom narrowed her eyes. "Do you want to find Wes or not?"

"Ok," I replied with an exaggerated sigh. I pulled up information for Arduba and tapped on city records. To my shock, a marriage certificate option popped up. Hesitantly, I tapped it. I scrolled down to the L's and was surprised to find a James Landon on the list. Wes never told me his dad's first name, but I clicked on it. James Landon and Allison Hardy, married twenty-two years ago. Wes would turn nineteen soon, so it made sense. I took a deep breath and switched over to the map of Illyria. Amante, a town just below Parthin stood out. I tapped on the little dot and pulled up the page of city information. The public listings option sat at the bottom of the page. My heart hammering in my ears, I scrolled down until I saw a Deborah Hardy.

"No way," I whispered.

"Find anything?" I looked up, startled. I'd completely forgotten mom in my search.

"Yeah…"

I told her what I found, then wrote down the address. It looked pretty close to the coast.

"I told you," she said with a twinkle in her eye.

The plan fell into place perfectly. It seemed foolproof, but mom...

"What if they come after you when they don't find me?"

"How can they? Hopefully they weren't listening, but even if they were I can just pretend that you told me you were headed back to the capitol and I had no idea what happened to you after that. Trust me, I play the part of worried-sick mom better than anyone."

For once, I didn't have an argument. "Are…are you sure you want me running away like that?" *Aren't you worried about me?* I thought sadly.

Mom's face melted into a worried frown. "Lily, I'll worry about you every day until I hear from you. But I would worry more if the Mainframe got their hands on you. I've known for so long that they would come for you one day and I should have done the right thing by sending you away. I was selfish. I didn't want to lose you because I'd already lost your dad, but I'm not giving in to weakness this time."

I pursed my lips. Like mom said, I'd be safer away from the Mainframe. They'd already forced Wes to run. And if they'd gotten to his parents…

I pushed the thought firmly from my mind. For the first time in days, I felt a fire burning in my heart. I had a purpose, a goal. I would find Wes and somehow we would work things out. Mom would be safe…for a time.

The doctor came in at that moment and smiled. "It's good to see you up and talking, Elaine. You'll be home in no time."

"Interesting you should say that," mom replied, looking carefully at me. "You've done so much for us, Dr. Thatcher, but would you be able to do one more thing?"

He looked back and forth between me and mom, his brow furrowed in confusion. Mom told him the situation in hushed tones and I watched as his eyebrows hiked further and further up his forehead.

"Um…you do realize that what you're asking me to do is *illegal*, right?" He strained his voice, clearly afraid of being heard.

"Yes…but we have no one else we can trust. Please help us."

He looked at me hesitantly. "Well…I don't really know what drug they used. If it's a standard paralysis drug, it should wear off within about ten minutes. She wouldn't really need an antidote."

For an instant, I felt like an idiot. Hot, boiling anger swept through me. Vic purposely acted like the paralysis would permanently paralyze me until the Mainframe people came. I wanted to punch him in his oily face. He'd made it sound like they could trace my whereabouts even if I took off the bug, but how could they? He'd probably lied about everything!

"What do you think?" Mom said. I looked at her, suddenly shaken from my angry reverie.

"I...I guess." I looked at the doctor. "Can you stand by? Just in case?"

Dr. Thatcher shrugged uncomfortably, clearly caught between the law and his natural tendency to help people in need. I swallowed hard and reached for the bug.

"Mom...you'll have to call. It'll sound more realistic if you call and act all frantic. Just say it came off accidentally when I tripped and fell, and tell them I can't get up."

Mom got her communicator out, poised and ready to call. I took a deep, shaky breath and reached up to my neck. I found the edge of the tracking bug with my fingernails and pulled. A brief burst of pain flashed down my spine before I collapsed.

Chapter Twenty-Four

My breathing quickened as a strange numb wave coursed through my body, spreading from my neck down into my torso and finally out to my fingertips and toes. I lay there on the cold floor, staring up at the bright lights of the ceiling. I tried to move a finger and couldn't. It worked so fast…

"Lily, I'm calling." Her voice stayed so quiet I could barely hear it over the fierce pounding of my heart. I swallowed the egg-sized lump in my throat and forced myself to be calm.

"Defense Department, please, it's an emergency!"

"Lady, do you know how many calls we get claiming emergency?"

"I need to talk to Defense! NOW!"

I had no problem hearing mom now. She must have acted in school plays or something because she pulled off hysterical mother better than anyone I knew.

"Ma'am, we-"

The woman got cut off, and for a moment all I could only hear silence.

"Are you Elaine Mitchell? This is her communicator." Vic's voice came over the speaker and I could just picture sleezy oil seeping from her communicator just from him talking into it.

"Yes, I'm Elaine, and my daughter's tracker came off when she fell and she can't move. What in the hell did you put in that thing? You better tell me or I'll hunt you down and make you wish you'd never been born!"

I had to stop myself from laughing. Not only had I *never* heard my sweet, gentle mother talk like that, but I'd certainly never heard her curse. She could definitely act. *Really* well. If I wasn't so terrified about being paralyzed, I would have thought it more funny.

"Excuse me, madam, but you will not address a superior officer in the Mainframe as such!"

"I'll address you however I like! You people have put my daughter in danger and so help me, you won't hear the last of it for days!"

"Uh…" I could tell Vic didn't know how to respond. He definitely wasn't expecting this. "The tracker could not have fallen off, Mrs. Mitchell. It's designed to attach firmly to the skin so that nothing can loosen it."

"You must not have put it on right, you idiot!" Mom practically shrieked now, and I could tell from the shuffle of footsteps nearby that people crowded by the door to watch. I heard someone's footsteps close by.

"Sir, it's true, she took a pretty bad fall and smacked her back against a table. I'm checking her over right now." I felt a gigantic rush of gratitude to Dr. Thatcher, risking his own life to make our story more believable.

"Mrs. Mitchell, you need to calm down!" came Vic's greasy voice "I informed your daughter of the paralysis effect, it is only in place to keep AWOL soldiers from escaping! It will wear off, at which time she will need to reattach it!"

"When is it going to wear off?"

"In about twenty minutes!"

Both shouted now, and if I could have laughed, I would have. Who knew that mom would be the only one to make the slimeball freak out?

"When it wears off, I will send an officer from the Ithaca branch of the Mainframe to reattach…"

He cut off just then and I heard mumbling in the background. My eyes grew wide in panic. Mom probably felt the same way. A Mainframe officer would make sure it attached and never came off. I would be trapped again.

I forced myself to shut down the feeling of panic when I heard Vic's voice again. "It seems that in light of recent events, all officers from Mainframe branches have been called to the capitol."

Recent events? What did he mean? Then suddenly it hit me. The break-in. It would make sense, they'd want as much back up as possible.

"Just…reattach it when the paralysis wears off, ok? All you have to do is push it to her skin and wait for the click. I don't have time to deal with this right now."

I heard the beep of the hang up and took a deep breath to steady myself. Mom rustled out of her sheets and stood over me with a huge smile on her face.

"I was worried there for a minute, but I think we're ok." She looked up and smiled.

"Thank you, Dr. Thatcher."

He didn't respond, so he must have nodded. I felt extreme pity for him. We'd kind of forced him into this situation.

"If they come looking for her, please just tell them she went on the morning train to Arduba." Mom pleaded softly now, once again her sweet self instead of the screaming psycho she'd been on the communicator to Victor.

Dr. Thatcher didn't respond. He must have nodded because mom looked reassured. He walked across the room to shoo away the onlookers, then appeared suddenly over my head.

"Lily? Can you move?"

"No," I responded, surprised I could still talk. My face didn't feel completely numb, just a bit like rubber. Whatever sicko thought this system up must have been a piece of work. How could you paralyze someone against their will, make them lay there lifelessly? I felt a surge of hate for Victor, the Mainframe, everything.

I felt hands under my arms and tried to jump in surprise, but couldn't.

"I'm going to move you to a bed." Dr. Thatcher. His voice sounded warm, full of concern. He got an arm behind my back and one under my knees. With a little difficulty, he put me on the bed next to mom.

"It'll probably hurt when it wears off since you slapped the floor pretty hard. I guess we should have thought to put you somewhere more comfortable."

I tried to shrug, and remembered I couldn't. I smiled weakly instead. "It's ok, it wouldn't have looked as convincing."

He smiled, but his eyes betrayed the nervousness he felt. "I'll check back in about fifteen minutes."

He walked out, his thick soled shoes squeaking on the tile. Just then, I felt a tingle in the tips of my fingers. I flexed a couple times and realized I could move my fingers a little. I scooted my hand slowly over to mom's hand and tried clumsily to squeeze her hand, to reassure her.

"Are you ok?" she asked.

"Yeah. I think some of the feeling is coming back."

"I'm sorry, Lily."

I began to wiggle my toes a bit. "Why?"

"I feel terrible. About everything. This mess, my cancer, the Mainframe…it just hasn't been fair to you. Some way to end high school."

I frowned, but my forehead didn't crease like it usually did. It felt very weird. "Mom…it's ok," I told her. "It's not your fault any of this happened."

"Yes, but I could have prevented a lot of it." She sighed deeply. "I just hope this can be a new start. You and Wes will at least have each other."

"What do you mean?" The tone in her voice worried me, one of sadness and calm.

"I mean, this is your chance to survive, Lily. I won't let you become the Mainframe's puppet."

"I know, mom, but I'm coming back for you. Once Wes and I have figured something out, we'll find you and his family and take everyone away from Arduba."

She sat up and faced me. "Lily, you can't ever go back to Arduba, even when I go back. Swear to me that you won't."

I tried to sit up, but my body hadn't fully woken up yet. "I have to! Who will take care of you?"

She smiled sadly and cupped my cheek in her hand. "Honey, you've already taken care of me. I'll get better. I'll live a long life. Maybe I'll even stay here in Ithaca permanently, if things work out. It's my turn to take care of you, and get you somewhere safe like I should have done years ago."

The numbness didn't stop tears from sliding down my cheeks and dripping off the sides of my chin. "Don't you want me to stay with you?"

Her chin trembled slightly as she nodded. "Of course I do, Lily. You're my baby." Her voice broke. "But I can't let them take you."

She leaned down and hugged me. I felt dumb, not being able to hug her back, but it didn't matter. I'd lost so much…now I had to lose mom? Everything inside me went numb too.

"I can't, mom. I can't promise you that I won't come find you when it's safe."

"Honey…"

We lapsed into silence, neither of us knowing what to say. The doctor came in a while later and smiled nervously.

"Let's see if some of that numbness has worn off," he said. I hadn't even tried to move. I didn't want to.

He moved my arms and legs, asking if anything hurt. After about five minutes, he asked me to stand up. I wobbled a little bit as I got on my feet, but soon I walked around the room, completely back to normal. I smiled and thanked him, but still felt hollow inside. How could I force myself to walk away from mom tomorrow morning, maybe forever?

I looked back at her, her eyes a little red and puffy from crying, and decided right there and then that I'd find her, no matter what. Nothing, not even the Mainframe, would stop me from keeping her safe.

Chapter Twenty-Five

The next morning revealed a cover of clouds, the wind a little chillier than a summer wind should be. As we stood outside, waiting for Annie to come pick mom up, I felt like a small, heavy brick lodged itself between my stomach and heart. Mom would drive away with strangers and then I'd be off to the train station. I clutched the tracker firmly in my hand. Dr. Thatcher thought there might be a device in it to detect skin contact, but as long as I held it in one hand it should be ok. We couldn't take any risks. At least, not until I got to the station.

Mom held my hand tightly, neither of us wanting to let go of each other. The memory of the goodbye with Wes surfaced in my mind, making me even more miserable as I stared at the sidewalk. I hoped against hope I'd find him in Amante, but who knew how long he'd stay at his grandmother's? Who knew if I even had the right place? Or person? All my uneasy thoughts raced through my brain, making me sick. I clutched mom's hand like a lifeline, the way I did as a little girl.

A sleek, black car pulled up and an extravagantly dressed blonde woman hopped out of the driver's seat once the door slid open. She looked very short next to mom and I, and her blue eyes twinkled mischievously.

"Elaine! It's so good to see you!"

They hugged each other, shrieking and laughing. Annie took mom's small bag and ran to the trunk to stow it. Then she ran to me, hobbling on tall, sparkly heels. Annie and her husband had lots of money, by the looks of it. I felt a little better about letting mom go to people I'd never even heard of.

"And this must be Lily…of course I got the birth announcement, but you were tiny back then!" She giggled and pulled me into a tight hug. I managed a smile back when she pulled away.

"Thank you again, Annie. I'm sorry it's so short notice." Mom smiled gratefully.

"Oh, don't worry about it at all! I'm so glad you called, I've been so bored lately. My daughter's always busy with her lessons and Tom is always at work! I'll finally have someone to talk to and go shopping with!"

She laughed again. Part of me wondered if her daughter took lots of lessons on purpose, just to get away from her loud, fluttery mother. Mom laughed along, but she looked subdued. She probably felt as scared as I did about saying goodbye.

"Well, come on, the cook's getting lunch ready as we speak! Are you sure you'll be ok, Lily? I can't believe you're old enough to be working and making your own way! Seems like yesterday we were that age, eh Elaine?"

Mom smiled and nodded distractedly. Annie stepped down from the sidewalk and clicked mom's door open. She slid into her own seat on the driver's side and honked loudly, startling me.

"Good to see you, Lily darling! Hope we'll see you again soon!" I smiled and waved awkwardly and turned back to mom, my heart sinking into my stomach.

"I'll try and get word to you soon. I've heard of people being able to talk on illegal channels," mom whispered. I wanted to tell her we could, that I'd forgotten to tell her Wes's mother had contacted me that way, but I couldn't speak around the lump in my throat. I smiled sadly.

"Lily, it's ok, we'll see each other again." Mom obviously tried to convince herself more than me. "We will. I…what I said yesterday, I just didn't want you to risk your life looking for me. When I move from Annie's, I'll get word to you somehow. Ok?"

I nodded, feeling the same way I felt when mom told me about her diagnosis, that things would work out, that we'd always be together. And it had, but I couldn't shake the haunting feeling that it would be a long time before I'd see her again.

Mom pulled me into a hug, triggering my tears. I clung to her, sobbing, never wanting to let go. The rational part of my mind screamed at me to hold it together, to hide my pain so I could focus on escaping from the Mainframe and finding Wes, but how could I cling to reality when I didn't know when I'd see mom again?

We finally let go, and mom wiped away tears from her own eyes. "I love you, honey. Be safe and remember the plan."

"I love you too, mom," I managed to choke out. "I will."

Mom kissed my cheek, squeezed my hand and climbed in the car. She drove away, her hand waving out the window. I watched until the car turned out of the parking lot and disappeared down some main road.

I wiped my tears furiously. I had to get under control and find my way to the train station. The hospital personnel gave me directions, but I couldn't afford a cab. I'd spent all of our extra on some supplies for me and groceries for mom to take to Annie's. So I would walking.

The day soon warmed up as the sun came out, making me sweat gallons. The air felt so much drier and hotter than it did in the capitol.

After about two miles, I saw the familiar station. Several more people crowded around the trains now, people headed to work or appointments or errands. Normal people, not like me.

I took a deep breath and clenched my hands around the ticket in my pocket. I scanned the station, looking for the train that read "Arduba" on it. I finally found it and hurried over. The digital board read ten minutes to departure. Perfect.

My hands began to sweat with fear. I scanned the station again for the train that read "Northern Cities," finally spotting it at the other end of the station. The Northern Cities train left a few minutes after the Arduba train.

Trying to look nonchalant, I strolled over to the Arduba train, pretended to peer at the schedule and hopped on. I took a seat, my breath coming out in small, nervous puffs. I slowly unclenched the hand that held the tracker and dropped it gently on the seat. I sat for a minute longer, feeling like every passenger on the train stared at me. I nudged the tracker back until it wedged between the back rest and the seat.

Carefully, I took out my ticket and frowned, rehearsing the act I'd planned since last night. I forced a look of surprise, then concern. My plan played out perfectly, until the train doors closed suddenly. But why? The train would leave at 10:40, but my watch read 10:35. I knew I'd gotten on the train for the capitol, and I'd made sure I had enough time to drop the device. Did Victor somehow find out the plan? Had he been in the hospital, watching me? No, he couldn't have, he had to deal with the break-in and the draft.

I looked up in alarm. The ticket takers paced the aisles, making sure everyone had a proper ticket. Any moment, I expected to see a burly Mainframe officer come barreling into my compartment screaming my name, but nothing happened. Frantic, I looked back up at the schedule. This one said the Arduba train left at 10:35, but it should have left at 10:40. I peered closer and noticed that the Arduba train B left at 10:40. I'd gotten them mixed up!

I tried to swallow down my panic, but I couldn't. My heart raced as the ticket takers came closer. But maybe I still had time. I could get up, get down the aisle, talk to the ticket taker, explain the situation.

I got up, ready to go, no longer scared, until the train gave a sudden jolt and began to move.

Chapter Twenty-Six

My mind raced furiously, searching for a way to stop the train. In old times, people could pull on some kind of pulley and the train would stop immediately, but they banned those years ago when people abused them. I got a sudden idea.

Putting on the most pathetic face I could, I staggered over to the ticket taker. He looked at me in alarm. Good. I'd put him on guard.

"I think I'm going to throw up," I gasped. "Can you stop the train?"

"Our car isn't anywhere near the conductor." He winced as I held my hand over my mouth.

"Please…I need to get off. It…it gets bad when I puke."

The man started to look a little green himself. "Ok, ok, I'll see what I can do, just…hold it down or something."

I knew I looked stupid, but I couldn't think of any other way to get off the train. He ran over to a phone, punched in some numbers on a keypad and swung open the plastic case that covered it. He dialed some number, yelled frantically about puking and other passengers and hung up. Beads of sweat ran down my temples as I waited for something to happen, but the train just gathered speed. Then, with a loud grinding noise, the train gradually slowed to a stop. The ticket taker swiped a security card through a slot and opened the door. I stumbled out with a hasty thank you and pretended to run to the nearest trash can. Luckily, we hadn't even left the station yet.

I pretended to lose my breakfast in the trash can, making disgusting noises and wiping my mouth occasionally.

"Ma'am?" I looked behind me to see the ticket taker standing by the train doors. "Are you coming?"

I shook my head. "Too sick," I called, impressed by how weak I sounded. Considering all that happened in the past forty-eight hours, I probably could pass for sick. "I'll catch a later one!"

He shrugged and stepped back inside the train. The doors closed and the train took off a moment later, snaking down the tracks away from the station.

"Northern Cities leaving in five minutes," came a bored voice over the intercom. "All passengers must board now."

I pretended to hunt for the bathroom to clean up so that onlookers wouldn't get suspicious. When everyone had stopped staring, I walked quickly to the other side of the station to a digital ticket changer, hoping no one had heard or noticed me. I inserted the ticket, changed the destination and printed a new one for the northern cities. As soon as I got to the train, gave my ticket to the ticket taker standing by the doors and hopped aboard. Thankfully, this train held far less people than the Arduba train. I found a seat near the back where I could sit unnoticed and unwind.

Before I could gather my wits, I started crying harder than I'd ever cried in my life. My whole body shook with the force of the sobs. So many jumbled thoughts chased each other through my mind-saying goodbye to mom, the first time Wes kissed me on the pier, the haunting letter from the Mainframe…it only took a matter of weeks for my life to fall apart. So much for planning to veg all summer and start at the university in the fall. My heart gave a strange lurch as I remembered the disk-like tracker that now sat on the Arduba train. How long would it take for them to discover that the tracker didn't move to get off? Or, if Dr. Thatcher was right and the bug had a heat sensor, did they already know that I'd left?

As my tears finally subsided, I stared out the window since I had nothing else to do. The countryside we passed through took my breath away. Lush, green, beautiful…it looked even more exotic and wonderful than Ithaca. The mountains here rose much higher compared to the ones at home. They towered over the train like sentinels, stern grandfathers with pure white hair of snow left over from winter. The train headed towards the mountains, getting ready to snake through a small canyon carved between the monstrous peaks.

For a moment, I forgot my pain and tears as the train entered the tall, vast walls of the canyon. I gazed up in wonder, staring at smooth, multicolored rock cutting off sharply into steep, pointed cliff tops. Some of the walls even held deep caverns, carved from years of water erosion. I'd never seen anything so breathtaking in my life. I leaned farther over the window sill and saw a small, light blue ribbon of water running along the bottom of the cliff beside the road. A river. I'd never even seen a river before.

Gradually, the gigantic cliff walls sloped gently down to the ground until the landscape turned from reddish rock to a huge valley. The river grew wide across, cutting a stripe of blue through the vivid green. I'd seen grass before, but this grass looked so strange. It rippled and flowed like the ocean waves I'd grown up with. Row after row of neat green plants flashed past the window, making it nearly impossible to see any individual row. I wanted to ask why the grass seemed so different, but I couldn't expose myself at any cost. I settled for staring in wonder at the beauty of it all.

Near noon, the conductor came over the intercom and started announcing cities. I knew Amante was farther north than Dorsi or even Parthin. Sure enough, the conductor announced Dorsi first.

My stomach rumbled, so I pulled out one of the packets of crackers I'd bought at the little convenience store near the hospital the day before. Mom had been with me then , walking, laughing, talking…acting like her normal self. The way she'd been before the diagnosis. Tears rose in my eyes and the crackers suddenly felt dry in my mouth.

Parthin came next. I tried hard to push down my bitter disappointment. If it hadn't been for the Mainframe, mom could have gotten better. I might have gone to college after all, since her treatment worked. But then, without the Mainframe, I wouldn't have had the money. The irony made me want to scream.

I leaned against the cool window a while later and felt my eyes drooping. I hadn't slept very well the night before. I'd laid awake, thinking about mom, how I would miss her, how things were finally back to normal and I couldn't stay with her. I clamped my eyes shut, forcing the memories out. I settled for thinking about Wes instead, remembering how he'd told me he loved me, how he'd kissed me, wrapped his arms around me…

"Miss?"

The voice seemed to come from a long way off, and yet it sounded urgent. Probably had something important to tell.

"Miss?" The voice sounded more impatient this time. I felt a hand on my shoulder, gently shaking me.

As I opened my eyes, I saw a frail looking, older man with wispy white hair. He wore a worried frown as I stared up at him vaguely. I gasped, remembering the day's train ride. As I shook the sleep out of my eyes, I realized everything looked different. The sun, so high in the sky a moment ago, had dipped very close to the horizon.

"I'm sorry, I must have fallen asleep," I mumbled. "I need to get off in Amante."

"We just passed through. We're in Cavri, and it's the last stop on the line. We're turning around to go back to Ithaca."

My heart froze. "Cavri? How far is that from Amante?"

"Half hour or so by train, but close to an hour by car."

I jumped up, dizzy and panicking. How could I have been so stupid? I wrung my hands uselessly.

"Can I ride the train back? Just to Amante?"

He gave me a long look. "I'm sorry, ma'am, but policy doesn't allow it. We have to clean the train before we head back into the city. All passengers have to get off."

I clutched my bag to my chest, praying to wake up again for real. It had to be a nightmare, being stranded far from Amante in a strange, small town near dark where I didn't know anybody. Who knew if cabs or anything ran from Cavri this time of night?

"Do you know how I could get to Amante?" I asked, trying to keep my voice calm.

He scratched his chin. "There might be a bus station. It's about a half-mile walk into town from here."

My heart sank. I probably didn't have enough money to get on a bus, especially for an hour. For that matter, I couldn't afford a cab either. I'd checked just this morning and I only had about twenty dollars in my bag. It might be enough to cover the cost, but most likely not.

"Or you can wait for the morning train, if you have somewhere to stay," he offered.

"No…my family's in Amante," I muttered. "I'll be fine. Thanks for your help."

I numbly walked out of the open doors and stepped onto the platform. I figured I should be crying, completely panicked and out of my mind, but I felt oddly calm. Either that, or I'd already worn out my tear ducts on the train.

I headed down the platform, following street lights down a small road. I'd never been in a place so eerily quiet, so different from home in the city where the noises never stopped. I walked quickly, shivering despite the warm evening air. I kept my eyes down, hanging on to hope about the bus, determined to make it to town before the sun went down. Soon, though, it fully disappeared behind the mountains by the time I reached the town center. Everything looked pretty much deserted, minus a small grocery store and…I couldn't believe my eyes, a bus station!

I hurried over, praying again and again that the small booth stayed open. Amazingly, a man stood inside, just reaching up to pull the cover down over the window. I heard the distant roar of a bus engine revving to life.

"Wait!" I hollered, running frantically, waving my arms like a maniac. "Please don't close up yet!"

The man looked up and huffed impatiently, making it clear that he did not want another customer at this hour.

"How much are tickets?"

"How far you going?" His face reddened as he glanced down at his watch, obviously angry, but I didn't care. I refused to stay in this hick-town all night, not when I'd come so far to Wes and safety.

"Amante," I panted. I clutched at the stitch in my side as I tried to catch my breath.

"Twenty-five."

I fought the urge to completely lose it. How could I have escaped the Mainframe, gotten mom to safety, found Wes's relative just to end up here, stuck in a bus station in the middle of nowhere?

"I have twenty…please let me on the bus, it's important!" I pleaded.

"It's twenty-five dollars, ma'am. Unless you have that, you can't get on."

"Please! You don't understand, I have to get on this bus! I *have* to!"

"Look, lady, I want to go home. My wife has dinner on the table and I don't want to stay here all night. Five more dollars or no go."

Tearfully, I opened my wallet and dug into the coin section, hating myself for buying the extra Danish at the bakery across the road from the hospital. I dug out a couple quarters, but it only came up to seventy-five cents. I held it pitifully up to the man, but he shook his head and closed the cover on the window, completely ignoring my protests.

"I've walked a mile to get here! The train won't let me on! GIVE ME A TICKET, YOU SELFISH JERK!" I pounded on the window cover until bruises started to form on my hands, but he didn't reconsider. The window cover stayed down, shutting me out from my last chance. Wes would undoubtedly move tomorrow, and I'd never see him again. I'd never see mom again. Overwhelmed, I sank down to the ground in despair.

Chapter Twenty-Seven

"Miss?"

I rubbed my head, trying to ignore the fact that I now heard voices. I just wanted to sit and ignore the world right now.

"Excuse me, Miss?"

The voice again. I supposed I might as well look up again and see if someone actually stood there, talking to me. I glanced up to see a middle aged woman with friendly smile lines around her lips and worried eyes.

"Are you ok?"

I stared at her dazedly. "No…"

"Where are you headed?"

"Amante. I have…family there."

The woman frowned, then turned around. "George?"

She called to some random person near her. A man approached, probably her husband, looking slightly older than the woman.

They talked in whispers for a minute, the man frowning at first, then his face falling in sadness. As their whispers died down, they glanced down at me, both of their faces now drawn in the same sad expression.

"Do you need a ticket?"

My eyes widened in disbelief. "A bus ticket?"

"Yes. We couldn't help but hear you um, talking to the bus clerk and thought you needed some help. We planned to visit family in Parthin, but we can get a ticket for the morning and go then. Amante is on the way, I'm sure the driver will stop for you."

"Are…are you sure?" I stammered.

The woman smiled sadly. "We're sure."

She held out a ticket. I could hear the rumble of the bus behind the station and knew I had only minutes, but how could I just take the ticket and run?

"No, I can't," I finally said after a fierce internal struggle. "I couldn't just do that."

"Please, we insist." George finally spoke up. "We…we had a daughter who looked a lot like you. She passed away a couple years ago in an accident."

The man's voice broke and he turned away. The woman nodded soberly and shook the ticket in her hand. "We couldn't stand to see you in trouble. Please take it, we want to help."

I stood up slowly and dug in my pocket. The dirty, rumpled twenty still sat there. I took it out and held it to them.

"I know it's not the right price, but please take this as payment."

The woman shook her head stubbornly. "No, this is on us. You need it more than we do."

I slowly took the ticket and felt tears welling up in my eyes. I hugged George, not really knowing why. Maybe because he'd been so generous, or because of his expression, or both. I hugged the woman next and thanked them profusely. They ushered me to the bus and helped me get on. The couple even stayed to explain the situation to the driver, who thankfully seemed more kind than his co-worker.

I plopped wearily down in an available seat and pushed the button to roll down the window.

"Thank you!" I called as the couple walked slowly towards the booth. They turned and waved, smiling but still sad. I sat down and leaned back against my seat, overwhelmed with gratitude.

A few more passengers filtered onto the bus before it finally took off. I looked at the time on my communicator. Eight o'clock. I reached in my pocket for another crumpled piece of paper, the paper that had the address of Wes's grandmother.

Even though I still felt exhausted, I forced myself to stay awake, listening intently for the bus driver to announce Amante. We arrived in Amante about an hour later, just as the ticket taker said.

As I stepped down from the bus, I felt my heart fill with hope for the first time in what seemed like years. Amante charmed me instantly with its beauty, a tiny town nestled in small foothills right next to the coast. I even saw the ocean down a narrow, twisting lane that led from the bus stop.

Only then did I realize I had no idea where to go. I turned back quickly to the bus and asked the driver about the address. He shrugged.

"I wish I could help, but I'm not from here. Sorry."

With that, he closed the door and started the engine. I asked some of the passengers who'd just disembarked with me, but all of them seemed in a hurry. I turned to a small, hunched-over woman with gentle eyes.

"Windswept Lane, that's just a couple blocks from here," she said in a rusty voice. She took a pen from her purse and drew out a quick map on the back of my paper.

"Thank you ma'am," I replied. I clutched the map in my hand and started off down the narrow, winding road towards the beach. It led, just like the woman said, to a main street of sorts. I couldn't believe such a small road could be called the main road. The central strip in the capitol had seven lanes on each side, but this road didn't even have painted road lines. Though the big clock down the road read only a little after nine, everything already shut down for the night, even the small coffee shop across the street. For downtown at nine, it seemed pretty deserted. Oddly, I liked it that way. The less people out and about, the less I'd have to explain.

I hurried up the main road, which climbed a gradual hill. Another street turned to the left, according to the map, so I followed it and came to a small lane barely large enough for one car. It ran along a foothill that faced directly out to the ocean.

I drew my breath in sharply, marveling at the scene before me. The moon just started to rise over the turbulent ocean, casting sparkling silver rays over the churning water. The hill sloped gently down from the road to the beach. Instead of the smooth sands like the beaches at home, these beaches were rocky, pebbly and cold. Gigantic rocks stood farther out in the water like silent guards, keeping the ocean from getting too rough. It looked different, but beautiful in an peculiar sort of way.

I stared for a while longer until I remembered how close I might be to Wes. Tearing myself away from the beauty of the landscape, I flew down the road towards the only house. It sat at the end of the lane, a small house battered by sea and wind. My heart grew lighter and lighter the faster I ran, making me feel like I could fly. The nightmare of the past twenty-four hours seemed to disappear as I imagined seeing him, holding him again.

I ran up the sagging, wooden porch to the door and stopped for breath. As soon as my heart rate slowed, I knocked loudly. A few minutes passed with no answer. I knocked again, anxiously. I hadn't seen a car anywhere near the property, but it might be in a garage. Or maybe his grandmother didn't drive anymore.

I rapped harder on the door, biting my tongue to keep myself from yelling out his name. Someone had to answer. I hadn't come all this way just to be disappointed. I pounded the door again, feeling the hope that welled so quickly inside me start to drain away.

"Just a minute! I'm an old lady and I can't walk very fast!"

I stopped knocking and stepped back as if I'd been hit. The voice startled me from my desperation. Finally, the wooden panels creaked open slowly and a woman in her eighties peered out. She didn't have a friendly face like the woman at the bus station. Her lips twisted up into a scowl.

"Who are you? What kind of person disturbs an old woman's peace this time of night?"

My heart sank. "Are...are you Deborah Hardy?"

"Yes," she snapped. "And I don't like to be disturbed."

"I'm so sorry, ma'am, but I'm desperate," I started, but before I could say anything else, she slammed the door in my face.

A sob rose in my throat before I could stop it. How could this cruel woman be related to someone like Wes? I fought the temptation to break the door down. Maybe he'd already left.

"Ma'am, please, I'm looking for Wes Landon!" I hollered as loud as I could, knowing she probably didn't hear too well. To my shock, the door flew open so fast that it banged against the wall behind it. I stumbled back again, amazed that I hadn't fallen off the rickety steps yet.

"I don't know who Wes Landon is! Get out of here!"

"But..."

She started to close the door again, but I reached out and grabbed it. She pulled back, surprising me with her strength.

"I'm not with the Mainframe! I'm his girlfriend!" It sounded desperate and lame, but maybe she would believe me. "My name is Lily Mitchell. I'm trying to find him. We're both fugitives, you have to believe me!"

"A likely story," she sneered. "Besides, I have no clue what you're talking about. Get off my property now! I've a shotgun and my husband taught me well how to use it!"

Something inside me crumbled into nothingness. The woman obviously had no idea about Wes. She probably didn't even know about the Mainframe. How could I have been so stupid? Coming on this wild goose chase, with half a chance of finding Wes?

She closed the door as I walked reluctantly down the steps and headed up the lane to nothing. I tried desperately to figure out my next step, but my brain felt as tired as my legs.

Suddenly, I heard a loud slam behind me and instinctively ducked. Footsteps pounded up the path towards me. I stood up, fearful that the old lady decided to come after me, but what I saw made my heart stop beating altogether.

"Lily?"

He stood there in front of me, a real person, not a vision or a hallucination. He gazed at me in a way that washed away the haunting anxiety riddling every part of my body. I rushed to him, let him fold me in his arms.

"Wes!" I wanted to cry, out of joy, relief, fear, everything, but I couldn't. I just held on to him, praying that he wouldn't disappear, that I really clung to him. He pulled back and looked down into my eyes, his face filled with relief, terror and intense love all at the same time.

"You found me," he whispered.

"I said I would, didn't I?" I smiled up at him and stroked his cheek. He hadn't shaved in what looked like several days. And then we kissed, his hands moving down my back to my hips, then up again to my face. He lifted me off my feet, twirling me around as he pulled away.

"I have so much to tell you…but let's not worry about it now." His deep, husky voice sent shivers down my spine. I smiled, still breathing fast.

"Ok," I whispered back.

"Come meet gram." His face lit up with a smile. "Sorry about her attitude…we just have to be *really* careful."

"That's ok." I laughed from sheer relief. "I understand."

He led me back to the ramshackle house. Gram, as he called her, stood in the doorway, looking slightly embarrassed. I smiled disarmingly, hoping she knew I understood. She smiled back, looking completely different from the woman who'd yelled at me seconds earlier.

A moment later, we sat in a small dining room cramped with tons of knick-knacks. Wes bustled around getting some tea ready. I couldn't help but notice that his grandma still looked at me a little warily.

"I'm Lily." I offered my hand and she shook it gently.

"Nice to meet you dear. I'm Deborah, as you probably already know, but most people call me Deb."

I smiled politely, not knowing what else to say.

"I'm sorry about the scene I caused earlier," she continued. For a woman her age, she looked remarkably stout, as if she could handle anything. Wes probably tended the tea out of polite concern for his grandma instead of necessity. I couldn't help but feel a twinge of jealousy. I'd never known my grandparents. Mom's parents died long ago.

"It's all right," I replied. "Don't worry."

Wes arrived with the tea and set a steaming mug in front of everyone. No one talked while we drank. The hot liquid tasted faintly of peppermint and felt good going down. My weariness ebbed a little as Wes explained to Deb how we knew each other.

"Well, she certainly is beautiful. You've done well for yourself, boy."

I blushed as Wes gazed at me. "Yes, she is."

"But how did you come to Amante? You're from the capitol, aren't you dear?" Deb looked at me questioningly.

"I am, but…it's a long story."

"I think Lily could use some sleep, gram." Wes cleared the empty mugs and set them in the tiny sink in the adjoining kitchen. The house looked much bigger inside than out, but it barely had more room than my apartment at home. Everything felt snug and cozy, with several old treasures lying around on tables and in glass cases.

We stood up, getting ready to go downstairs, when my communicator suddenly rang. Wes looked at me in alarm.

"You still have your communicator?" His eyes grew wide with panic.

"Well…yeah. How else am I supposed to get in touch with mom?"

"They can trace it here! Didn't you ever think about that?"

I shrugged, too embarrassed to know what to say. I took out the phone and looked down to see a mail note from mom. I tapped the screen to open the message.

"Back in the capitol. Safe to come back and find me."

Chapter Twenty-Eight

I stared down at the message for what seemed like hours. Mom, back in the capitol? How could that be possible? I only left her this morning, even though it felt much longer.

"We have to destroy it. Now!"

I looked up to see Wes staring at me in a panic. "Destroy what?"

"The communicator! It's a direct link to the Mainframe. We have to cut all ties to the city, it's our only chance."

"But…" Rationally, I knew I had to, that Wes was right, but what if the message did come from mom? I could only connect with her if I had the communicator. I didn't know they could be tracking devices.

Before I could stop him, he took my communicator, threw it on the floor and stomped on it. The metal crumpled underneath his heavy boot.

"What are you *doing*?" I hollered indignantly. "I didn't even get a chance to see if that message was fake!"

"What message?" He stopped stomping for a minute and looked up at me.

"A message from my mom…she said she got back to the city and that I could go get her."

His eyes narrowed with suspicion. "How long ago did you see her?"

"I left her with a friend in Ithaca this morning."

He rubbed his stubbly chin. "It's gotta be a fake, Lil. Why would she message you so soon?"

"I don't know…she planned to stay with Annie for a while, but what if it's real? I can't just ignore her!"

"It takes three hours to get from Ithaca to Arduba, Lily." He shrugged. "If it is real, then I think she can wait for you until it really is safe for us to go back."

I thought about the way mom worried so badly that we'd never see each other again. She'd certainly made it sound like she wouldn't leave Ithaca anytime soon. And yet…

Wes took a deep breath and let it out. "Luckily, if they were tracking you, you probably weren't here long enough for them to figure out exactly where you are. Communicator signals get a little scrambled up here."

He did a double take, then looked at me intently. "Hey, what about your tracker? How'd you get rid of it?"

I sank wearily into a chair and put my head in my hands. So many thoughts ran through my mind that my head felt ready to explode.

"I took it off."

Wes's eyes grew wide with alarm. "What about the paralysis?"

"It worked." I smiled up at him wryly. "Mom and I thought up a plan to get rid of it."

Wes and Deb listened intently as I told them about removing the bug in the hospital, my brief bout of paralysis, taking the tracker with me to the train station and leaving it in the Arduba train while I transferred to the northern cities train. Wes cracked a smile when I told him about faking sick to get off the moving train. He occasionally interrupted with things like, "That creep! He made it sound like you were permanently paralyzed!" and "You're insane, Lil."

"Anyway," I finished, "hopefully they won't find me anytime soon."

Wes looked at Deb uneasily. "I hope not," he muttered darkly. "But just in case, we should probably move tomorrow. I don't want Gram getting hurt."

"Oh, Wes, quit worrying. You got rid of the communicator. We should be fine for a while yet. At least let the girl stay and rest for a day. You can leave day after tomorrow."

Wes shrugged while I nodded gratefully, too weary to talk anymore. He took the cue and ushered me to a small room at the back of the house. Deb brought in some extra sheets and blankets.

"Thank you," I said wearily. Since the house only had two bedrooms, Wes decided to sleep on the floor while I took the bed. The familiar flutter of anticipation and desire flared within me at the thought of sleeping in the same room, but I felt too achy to react to it as strongly as I had when Wes stayed in my apartment.

I'd brought pajamas in my bag, but I couldn't muster the energy to change into them. I slipped under the covers, fully clothed, and adjusted the pillow.

"Lily?"

Wes's voice sounded a little muffled. He rustled his sheets around a little and sat up.

"Yeah?"

"I'm glad you're here," he whispered.

"Me too."

The sound of the ocean soothed me as I fell asleep. I could almost imagine being home again, but I longed to stay in this place more than I'd ever wanted to stay in the city. I could actually hear the waves pounding against the shore. At home, the sound mixed with the occasional shout, beeping horns and the obnoxious laughter of drunks coming out of the bars at all hours. Life seemed so much less complicated here.

We both fell asleep quickly, neither of us waking until the rising sun shone through the window. I stretched comfortably, wanting to stay in this soft bed all day. My whole body creaked and groaned as if I'd just run a marathon.

Wes sat up, stretched and grinned at me. "I have to admit, I could definitely get used to waking up to your beautiful face every day."

I smiled back, too shy to let him know I felt the same way. His old self emerged again, completely different from the tense fugitive he'd been the night before.

We got up and headed to the dining room where Deb sat drinking a cup of black coffee. She smiled and waved us in, looking much more friendly today. I noticed her eyes matched Wes's almost exactly.

"I made breakfast." She gestured to three bowls of oatmeal with dried strawberries on top. I sat down and ate hungrily, realizing for the first time that all I'd only eaten a granola bar and some crackers yesterday. The strawberries tasted good, but I longed for fresh strawberries. I'd only tasted them once before.

We polished off the meal with a whole glass of milk each. I hadn't had milk much either, since grain had become so expensive and hard to grow. *Maybe they have more grain-fed cows up here,* I thought vaguely.

"Thought I'd include a little treat since you had such a rough day yesterday," Deb explained.

After breakfast, Deb set about scrubbing her house. Wes and I helped. It felt strangely surreal, cleaning everything with soap and water like they did in the old days. I'd never seen wood furniture or floors that had to be polished. Everything back home was made of chrome, plastic or linoleum. Usually, I just wiped a wet rag over the surfaces in our apartment. I got covered in sweat and worked my aching muscles even more, but I felt oddly satisfied.

Deb settled down for a nap later in the day, so Wes and I decided to walk on the beach. The sun warmed our backs, but the air here felt at least ten degrees chillier than it did at home. A strong breeze whipped up, tossing the waves to and fro.

"People probably don't surf much here, do they?" I asked. He strolled alongside me down the pebbly beach with an easy smile on his face.

"Not this part of the beach. A little farther south, there's a public beach. This little stretch from that cliff to the jetty over there is Gram's property, so she has her own private beach."

My mouth dropped in shock. I'd never heard of anyone owning so much land before. Mom and I only had our tiny little rented space. Most of the people in the city lived that way.

"Wow." I gazed out at the water lapping the shore and wished suddenly that I'd grown up here in a place like this, a place with friendly people, clean air and open land.

"Well, for a hideout, it's not bad." Wes grinned down at me. "It's a little different from home, but I love it here. I've only been here once, when I was really little. Mom and I came to visit when she and dad…well, never mind."

He looked a little worried when I glanced up at him, but quickly rearranged his smile when he saw me watching. We walked along a little farther, exploring the vibrant tide pools and the many coves along the shoreline. Wes picked a few beautiful wildflowers growing along the beach scrub and held them out to me.

"A late birthday gift," he said. "I know they're not much, but…"

He stopped as I flung myself into his arms and kissed him. His lips tasted like the salt air. This place felt like paradise, and being with Wes only made it better. If only we could go on like this forever, not worrying about the future or whether the Mainframe hunted for us.

Around noon, we went back up to the house and got some easy-to-carry food to take back to the beach. We dipped our toes in the cold water as we ate, enjoying the contrast between the icy water and the warmth of the sun.

"I've always wanted to live here," Wes said suddenly. "To me, it's the most perfect place on earth."

"It is," I agreed. "The beaches back home are nice, but I've never seen anything like this."

Wes shifted awkwardly in the sand. He looked nervous.

"What's wrong with you? Sand in your unmentionables?"

He laughed nervously and ran his hand through his curls. "No…I was just thinking about something."

"What?"

"Do you…ever think about us in the future? I mean like, being married?"

Chills crept up my back as I took in what he'd just said. He wanted to be married? To me?

"I mean, not now or anything," he mumbled hastily. "I just thought about how incredible it would be to stay here with you, maybe get married on the beach, live here, raise a family here…"

He trailed off nervously and leaned back against his hands. A warmth, far more beautiful than the sun's, spread through me. People didn't get married in churches with big ceremonies anymore, but I'd always dreamed of wearing a flowing white dress and promising to be with someone forever. I looked out across the sand and imagined Wes and I walking hand in hand, maybe even with a little girl and boy following behind…

"I would love that," I whispered, taking his hand in mine. A huge grin spread over his face as he looked at me.

"You would?"

"Of course."

He wrapped his arms around me and we sat contentedly, watching the waves, until Deb called down to us for dinner.

Deb outdid herself with a meal of real bread and butter, potatoes, noodles with some kind of sauce and a pie made from real peaches. But the salad really got my attention. A real salad, not the rubbery pasta salads with freeze-dried vegetables so common in the city. The huge bowl held crisp, green lettuce, plump red tomatoes and tiny sliced onions.

"Where did you get real tomatoes? And bread?" I asked the question before I could stop myself. I felt horrible, eating food that must have cost her a fortune.

She laughed. "Well, the effects of the Burial aren't as bad up here as they are in the capitol. But if you know how to treat the soil, you can grow things just fine."

"What do you mean?" My curiosity peaked.

"Laziness is the root of all of the Mainframe's problems. People just don't treat the earth the way it should be treated, and farmers are near non-existent now. When factories and machines completely took over food production, instead of individuals who had knowledge of soils and plants, that's when we went downhill."

I looked at her, trying not to look confused. "But…what do farmers have to do with anything?"

"The way you fix soil is by using plants. People had chemical spills even years ago, but they tested seeds and plants to figure out what could grow in tainted soil. In the process of growing, the plants got rid of toxins."

"Really?" The thought boggled my mind. How could people who lived so many years ago know so much more than us?

Deb laughed. "Come with me. Let me show you something."

She led us to the back of the house and opened a door to a huge yard. I stepped out, breathing in the sweet smell of fresh fruit, vegetables and something tangy I couldn't quite identify. Tomatoes sat in neat rows, along with rows of small sprouts. Another row held huge green things shaped weirdly like heads. Along the edge, a row of huge green stalks towered over the rest of the plants, almost as tall as Wes. I recognized golden corn hanging from the stalks. I'd seen pictures in history books of the plant. All around the garden, and even in patches throughout, sat bunches and bunches of some kind of purple flower. Scattered through the purple flowers were tall yellow flowers that looked almost friendly. In the far end of the yard stood a sturdy looking tree with golden peaches hanging from the branches. I breathed in the sweet smell again, marveling at the sight of so much fresh food.

"The purple stuff, or heather, helps the plants grow. Those plants been there for years, cleaning the soil, just after the Burial. The yellow ones are sunflowers. They're both hardy plants, and could handle the radiation. They cleaned everything up so I could grow other things. I've been growing food for about three years now."

I stared in shock. Why hadn't the Mainframe figured this out? The solution seemed so simple. Surely someone would have thought of this by now. Deb bent down and picked some scraggly flowers off of the green plants.

"Weeds," she explained, holding them up for me to see.

"But...how did you get the milk? And bread?"

She laughed again. "I'm good friends with a rancher down the road. He used the same trick and his cattle and cows stopped getting sick. I trade him vegetables and fruit for grain, meat and milk."

"Why doesn't the Mainframe do things like this? The city's in famine while the rest of Illyria is surviving just fine."

"I don't know," Wes muttered back. "But it would stop this stupid war. It would fix a lot of things."

He stood looking out at the garden, frowning and rubbing his chin. I had a feeling that the same idea that ran through my mind ran through his.

Chapter Twenty-Nine

The garden stunned me. Here in this little yard in the middle of nowhere sat more food than I'd ever dreamed could exist. I wondered how many other people away from the city had figured out how to cleanse the soil and were growing food. From the way Deb talked, it sounded like several people became self-sufficient here while people starved on the streets at home every day. The capitol, the center of our civilization. It made me shiver to think how degenerate people in the city had become, how the Mainframe had degraded everyone to the point of bitter despair. And now they wanted to send everyone to war for a solution they already had. Why were they so narrow-sighted? If they actually talked to citizens or created some kind of council, all these problems could be eliminated.

I tried to shrug off my uneasiness. The stars still hung low in the evening sky, so Deb set up a table on her back porch and taught us a few new card games. The decks were tattered, obviously old and used many times, but still good to play with. I'd only played cards once or twice in my life with neighbors in the apartment complex. People didn't buy cards a lot in the city because spare money usually went toward food. While we played, Deb told us stories about growing up on her parent's farm in the days when people still knew how to grow food.

"And one time, my mom was driving the truck behind my dad and brothers while they baled hay, and the shift came off in her hand," Deb explained, trying hard not to laugh. "So she tried to tell my dad, and he couldn't hear her over the engines. She finally grabbed the broken stick shift and waved it out the window. You should have seen the look on his face!"

All of us doubled over, laughing so hard that it hurt. I loved hearing her stories, but my laughter felt tainted with jealousy. Deb clearly never worried about thugs, or getting home before sunset, or staying in a dark apartment all day when blackouts covered the city. She'd probably never wondered how to put food on the table with just a small amount of spare money, or how to pay the rent and other little expenses with virtually no income. I even felt a little jealous of Wes. He'd at least been able to visit this place as a child and know a different life from the city. Besides, he knew his family. Mom and I only had each other. I tried to keep a smile on my face, but a sudden feeling of keen loneliness cast a shadow over the game.

We played cards long after sundown. Deb looked at the clock ruefully. "I guess we should turn in for the night," she said sadly. "What a shame, too. I haven't had this much fun in years."

I looked down at my lap, ashamed. I'd been so wrapped in my own anguish I hadn't even thought about Deb, living here alone, probably wishing for visitors every day.

Before bed, Deb packed us some extra food for our trip the next morning. That feeling of wistful sadness came over me again at the thought of leaving Deb's comfortable little house. I could relax here, let myself go, but the question of food still bounced around in my mind, making me restless. Wes and I could have a perfect life here, I could bring mom to this wonderful place, but we'd always have to run from the Mainframe. I tried to push my troubled thoughts away as I got ready for bed.

Wes slept on the floor again while I took the bed. I sank into the comfortable cotton sheets, but soon tossed and turned restlessly.

"Penny for your thoughts?"

Wes's whisper startled me out of my thoughts. "I just keep thinking about what your grandma said about food. Could it really be that easy?"

"You saw her garden." I could imagine him shrugging in the dark. "She's had food for years."

"Why doesn't the Mainframe do that?"

He sighed. "I don't know. I think they stick to the capitol. They don't venture out into the country unless they're collecting levies. Besides, the soil is worse around Arduba since that's where the burial happened."

"Yeah, but I'm sure plants would take care of the toxins after a while. Deb said it didn't take her that long. And in the meantime, we could import food from the north. It would fix everything."

"Well, like Gram said, maybe they're just lazy. Or ignorant. They don't know how to work with soil anymore since machines have done it for so long. Besides, the Mainframe doesn't like Northern Illyria much."

"Why?"

"They wanted to break off, secede a while ago. They probably saw where the country was headed and wanted out, but the Mainframe wouldn't allow it."

"That's so stupid!" I countered. "Let bygones be bygones and hire people from the country to work the soil!"

He sat up on his elbows and studied me with soft eyes. "I wish it was that easy, Lil. But they're all drones, these Mainframe people. They're so focused on this war that they're not thinking of alternatives. And they're not doing anything with the northern cities."

He yawned loudly, making me yawn too. I knew we needed sleep for tomorrow, but I didn't want the perfect day to end. Several hours passed before my troubled thoughts faded into blackness.

We woke early the next morning, before the sun came up. Wes reasoned that it would be better to travel in semi-darkness than broad daylight.

"Are you sure you have to leave?" Deb looked a little sad. I thought again how lonely she must be in this little cottage by herself. "I don't think they'll come looking for you. You took every precaution possible."

Wes looked at me uneasily before he turned back to her. He stooped down and kissed her on her withered cheek. "I wish we could. But I'm just looking out for you, Gram. Thank you for everything."

"Anytime, dear."

Deb gave me a hug and then poked Wes sternly in the chest. "If you let this young lady go, I'll give your ears a good boxing."

Wes laughed. "I won't let her go, don't worry Gram."

We left through the front door, after Wes ran through protocol with Deb again. He told her to say she'd never heard of Wes and if they persisted, they could investigate the house. As soon as we left, Deb would set to work washing and folding linens and clearing dishes to make it appear that only one person lived there.

"Where are we going?" I asked as we trooped down toward the beach, a couple bags slung across our shoulders.

"North," he replied, squinting against the rising sun. "We just have to get as far away from the city as possible. We'll find a lot more caves up here that we might be able to hide in."

We tromped on, pausing only to eat and drink every so often. After a while, I became aware of a faint noise above the roar of the surf, a strange rumbling combined with a weird beeping noise.

"Do you hear that?" I looked at Wes, my stomach tightening in fear at the look on his face. He definitely heard the noise and, judging by the terror on his face, knew it couldn't be good.

"It's radar," he whispered, his voice constricted with rage and fear.

"What?"

He pushed his finger to his lips and stopped walking. His eyes grew wide as he looked around for somewhere to hide.

"We've gotta get out of sight of the road." He squinted at the craggy cliffs, then grabbed my arm and pulled me around some beach scrub toward the rocky face. When we got up close to the cliff wall, he pointed to a tiny crevice.

"It won't fit us both," I choked. All the while, the roar became louder and louder until it almost deafened us. The beeps seemed to speed up, an ominous warning of doom. My stomach twisted. The Mainframe. Somehow, they'd tracked us down.

"Hurry, get in," he said tersely.

Before I could do anything, he'd shoved me into the small space. My arms scraped roughly against the opening of the small cave, but I finally managed to squeeze into the tiny hole and sit down.

"Now back up so you're not seen." I backed obediently as far as I could against the rock wall until I couldn't see him anymore. Wes started to squeeze in, but his shoulders couldn't fit.

"Hurry!" I hissed.

"I can't fit, I have to find somewhere else to hide," he gasped. "Just stay there. I'll come back, I swear."

He rushed off, leaving me to panic in the small cave. My protest died in my throat, making me feel strangled.

"Wes," I choked uselessly. "Come back!"

My voice sounded weak and whiny. I strained my ears as hard as I could, trying to figure out where he'd gone.

"Halt! By order of the Mainframe!"

My heart sped up so fast I thought it might explode. How could they see me? I'd been shoved into a rock! But the answering voice skyrocketed my terror.

"What seems to be the problem?" Wes spoke up loudly, sounding calm and confident.

"Hey...I know you! You're Wes Landon! You're in defiance of the draft!"

I stood up and started scrambling to get through the rock, but I felt like I moved underwater. Everything seemed to slow down.

"No, I'm not. I'm Justin Brickley. See, I have my ID right here."

Wow, he really did cover all his bases. How did he know how to get a fake ID?

"Yeah, right, son. Your picture's been posted all over Arduba since you failed to show up for the draft. You're comin' with us."

I scrambled vainly, trying to squeeze myself out of the rock. I had to save him, get to him before they could take him.

"You know, though, we got a call about Lily Mitchell, not you. The Mainframe traced her communicator signal here."

A new voice spoke this time, much rougher and frightening than the other. "Yeah, you know anything about her kid?"

"I don't know what you're talking about! My name is Justin Brickley and I live here!"

"Why you carrying a pack then, kid? You don't look like you're stickin' around," sneered the harsh-voiced one.

"I'm camping," Wes shot back. "Is that illegal now?"

"Well, 'Justin,' we're still going to have to take you in. I'm sure a little DNA test at the Mainframe won't scare you, will it?"

I scrambled desperately against the rock, unable to move my foot. The hem of my pants caught on a rough rock. I backed into the cave quickly to release it, then flung myself at the entrance again. They'd know about Wes as soon as those test results came back.

"Maybe he stole the girl's communicator to throw us off the trail," muttered the smooth-voiced man.

"Just the thing a fugitive would do."

"Come on, then. Vic'll be happy with an insubordinate at least."

"No, no!" I whispered uselessly.

"You're lucky, kid. Vic usually executes insubordinates, but he needs all the troops he can get."

"You're pretty much dead where you're headed, anyway."

My heart throbbed painfully in my chest. I'd made it halfway out of the cave, but I couldn't get my legs through. How had I gotten into this awful hole?

The two goons guffawed as I finally pushed my hips out of the narrow opening. So close, so close…

"What are you *doing*?" I heard a loud thump, followed by a grunt of pain. "Hurry up, this kid's trying to make a break for it. Help me get 'im on the rover."

I finally pushed myself out when the thundering rumbling started again. I held my hands over my ears, trying to block out the painful noise. I couldn't hear the beeping anymore. The roaring and grinding grew faint as I wearily pulled myself up with my scratched and bleeding arms. With a few staggering steps, I started running down the beach. A huge Mainframe vehicle, a rover, grumbled down the road. I ran after it, trying to keep pace, but the gigantic machine picked up speed and drove over a distant hill. They'd always moved so slowly in parades on the streets of the city. How did they go so fast now?

I didn't stop, just ran and ran, my breath coming out in ragged rasps. I finally caught sight of it driving up another hill and pushed my already burning lungs past the limit. They'd gotten him, but they couldn't take him. They couldn't…

The rover rounded one last bend, then disappeared completely. I collapsed on the sand, my bruised and battered legs unable to take anymore. He'd given himself away to protect me, and now he'd be shipped off to war. Or worse.

I pounded the sand uselessly with my fists. How could he have been so stupid? With no plan, no hope, I curled up in the sand and cried.

"Well, well, well…Lily Mitchell! Who would have thought I'd find you here?"

A voice, oily and full of hatred, oozed through my consciousness. I looked up slowly to see Victor Channing towering over me, a look of smug satisfaction on his slimy face.

Chapter Thirty

I stood up slowly, shaking all over with fear and rage. No way. After all this, I'd really been ambushed by Vic?

"Lily, Lily, Lily…it's not often that I grant special favors. And you took advantage of my kindness. I can't believe I actually fell for that whole bit in the hospital. You timed it just right with that weapons raid."

I just stared at him, hatred seeping through my veins. He trapped me, just like an animal. He'd drag me back to the capitol and enslave me in his army. Or worse. After all, I'd be considered insubordinate now.

"So what?" I spat. I tried to sound tough, but my voice came out a strange, small squeak.

"Oh, Lily, you're lucky I'm so kind," he said, taking out a pistol and shining the barrel on his sleeve. "I have a proposition for you."

"I'm not making deals with you!"

I kicked at him wildly, trying to get the gun out of his hands, but he caught me easily by the arm and held me. Without warning, a strange surge of heightened adrenaline shot through me, arching my back and twisting my arm. I let out a feral growl and shoved Vic away. The gun slipped a little before he caught it again and pointed it at me.

"I know what you are, you freak," he snarled. "But I also know that you can be shot. You're almost indestructible, but not quite."

He sounded tough, but looked very pale. I'd scared him, but I felt too tired and scared to fight. He smoothed his disgusting hair with one hand and relaxed a little.

"As I was saying, I have a deal for you."

I rolled my eyes in response.

"Come with us, or your boyfriend dies."

Fear gripped me, but I tried to tamp it down. "How do I know you're not lying? What if you've already…killed him?"

The words felt like poison on my tongue, but I didn't know what else to say. I had to stay level with Vic, not give in to hysterics like he wanted me to.

"Unlike *some* people, I keep my promises," he muttered. "And besides, I know you'll just run off unless I can compromise with you. And if you run off, I'd have to kill you, and then we'd never be able to test you and create our formula."

"Test me? For a *formula*?"

"As I'm sure your dear mother told you, your DNA is fused with the powers of Akrium, without the side effects. You're our only hope for building an army strong enough to defeat the south."

I snarled again. "If all this is about food, why don't you learn how to take care of the soil? That would fix the problem just fine."

A flicker of anger passed over his face, but he quickly forced himself to relax and laughed mockingly. "You teenagers, thinking you know everything. The soil is damaged beyond repair. This war is necessary if our country is to survive."

"People ar…" I stopped myself, not wanting to betray Wes's grandma or anyone else in this town, just in case they'd be incarcerated for it. "Whatever," I finished lamely.

"Drama, drama. Now please decide. Are you going to cooperate and let your precious Wes Landon live? Or are you going to insubordinate even further and end his life?"

He held up a small radio, placing his finger threateningly over the call button. "I have a direct link to the soldiers in the rover where he is. I can give them the order to shoot now."

I froze like a deer in headlights, as people used to say. Of course I'd never seen a real deer, but…what was I thinking? Why would I think about deer at a time like this? Vic must have noticed that my eyes glazed over because he lifted the radio.

"Fine!" I screamed. "I'll go! Don't kill him."

Vic smiled a greasy smile. "I thought you'd see things my way."

"I *swear*, if you kill him, I *will* kill you."

He smirked arrogantly, but it couldn't hide the small flare of fear in his eyes. No matter what he said, he knew what I could do. *I guess there are perks to being a mutant monster after all*, I thought bitterly.

Wordlessly, I followed Vic into the truck, my heart breaking more each step of the way. Yeah, I'd saved Wes's life, but would I ever see him again? That, along with all my other troubled thoughts, swirled through my mind as I climbed into the rover. At least I'd made sure mom would be safe. I clung to the thought, my only comfort. As far as I knew, Vic had no way of knowing where she went after she left the hospital.

"OW!" A sharp pain cut through my head as someone clubbed me with the butt of a rifle. It quickly wore off, as other injuries usually did, but it had still made my vision swim.

"Crooks, you idiot! I didn't give orders to club her! We need her intact!"

I heard a low thump and a moan, but I could barely focus on anything. My mind swarmed with thoughts of Wes, taken far away from me to who knows where. Even if they only sent him to war, they'd probably still dish out some kind of punishment. I wanted to scream and break every window in this ugly truck.

Vic sat in the driver's seat and revved the engine. He and the other soldier, Crooks, argued the minute they started back down the winding road. I leaned my head against the cool window glass and tried vainly to come up with some kind of escape plan, but my thoughts remained clouded. Eventually, I drifted off into an uneasy sleep, jerking awake several times from nightmares.

"Get up," said a rough voice behind me. I opened my eyes wearily and looked up to see the other soldier leaning over from the front passenger seat. I must have slept much longer than I thought, because when I stepped out, the sun set in the distance over the silhouette of the Mainframe building. We were back in the city.

Chapter Thirty-One

I figured we'd go into the Mainframe building, but Vic took me firmly by the shoulder and steered me to the right towards Biltmore prison.

"Why are you taking me to Biltmore?" I felt panic rising in my throat again.

"You didn't expect us to give you a five star suite, did you?" He laughed a harsh, raspy laugh. "You'll stay here the night, then we'll take you over to the Mainframe for testing in the morning."

I tried to wiggle away, terrified, but Vic clamped on tighter. I'd heard so many horror stories about Biltmore. One prisoner got so desperate that he'd found a way to break the knees of the guard standing outside the bars.

We walked through the double doors into some kind of lobby. A guard in an uncomfortable-looking uniform looked up and waved lazily when he saw Vic. A loud buzz sounded from somewhere, followed by an iron door opening before us. Behind the door were two halls that branched off diagonally. One said "Men" above the entry, and the other said "Women." I wondered wildly if Wes had been taken down the men's hallway.

As we entered the hallway, the other prisoners began to riot, pounding their fists on the bars and yelling. The women looked beyond scary, some with no hair and others with huge scars all over their faces. Vic led me to my cell, if you could even call it that. I stared into a damp, dark hole in the wall covered with bars. A small pallet sat in the corner, along with a tiny sink and a bucket that served as a toilet. I glanced at the cell to the right, shocked to see a woman at least fifty years older than me huddled in the corner, not yelling with the other prisoners. Something about this shriveled old woman intrigued me. What had she done to deserve Biltmore? How long had she been here? Before I could think much more about it, Vic roughly removed my handcuffs and shoved me in.

"Have a nice night," he laughed as he slammed the door and stalked down the hall to the entrance.

I swallowed hard, trying not to panic. I looked into the cell straight ahead, where a tiny but burly woman stood. Her eyes sunk deeply into her skull, giving them a hollowed look. She stared at me, her small fists clenched tightly around the bars. Her bright red, frizzy hair reminded me of a clown. She even had some bald patches.

"What're you in for?" she barked. I shook as if she'd hit me across the face.

"I...uh, I..."

"Do you talk?"

"It's a long story," I finally managed to stutter. "But I'm just in for tonight."

She spat on the floor in front of her cell. I couldn't help wrinkling my nose in disgust. I *hated* it when people spit. The crazy woman saw me and chuckled.

"Boy you are disgustingly squeamish, you know it?"

I sat down on my pallet, suddenly determined to not talk to her, praying she would just leave me alone.

"What's your name, kid?" she called.

"Alice," I replied, using the first name that popped into my head.

"Alice, huh? More like, a lice!" She guffawed loudly at her own joke. The grammar nerd in me wanted more than anything to tell her that "lice" is the plural form and the correct singular form would be "a louse," but my fear kept me quiet.

"Name's Janice," she said, picking her teeth with her bright red nails. A huge tattoo of a dragon on her arm showed up in the light. "I'd tell you what I got thrown in the clink for, but it'd probably make you have nightmares. Your mommy's not here to coddle you now."

I knew she baited me, so I stayed silent, trying not to play into her game.

"Strong, silent type, eh? Whatever, kid. Just stay outta my way in the grub line. I don't like to wait for my food."

Who do you think you are? I thought, trying to keep the disgust off my face. I pulled my knees to my chest and huddled down, trying to ignore her. She finally got the hint, belched loudly and lay on her small mattress at the back of her cell.

"You'll get used to Janice," said a soft voice nearby. I lifted my head slowly and turned to see the wrinkled face of the old woman next to the bars that divided our cells, the woman who hadn't rioted with the other prisoners.

"Really?" I whispered, throwing a cautious glace at Janice's cell. A loud snore sounded from her direction. "Is she always that crazy?"

"Yeah, she drives us all nuts," replied the woman. "The only quiet we have is when she's asleep, or when she passes out drunk from her smuggled liquor."

"She can smuggle…?"

"Don't ask," she replied, shaking her head slightly.

I giggled softly. "What's your name?"

"Agatha, but most people call me Aggie or Aggs."

"It's pretty," I replied.

"Thank you. I like your name too."

"Oh, Alice isn't my real name. I just didn't want Janice to know it."

"Well, what is your name?"

"Lily."

"Oh, even more beautiful," she said softly. "It reminds me of the fields in my home town north of here. Lilies bloom all summer long."

"You're from north country?" I asked. "What part?"

"Dorsi. It's nothing like here."

"Yes, I…passed through there recently," I replied, still unsure if I could really trust her. "How come you moved here?"

"I came when I turned sixteen or so. My father began working for the Mainframe, so we had to relocate here."

Aggs coughed loudly. Her jumpsuit had worn thin, and the blanket she'd draped over her shoulders wasn't much thicker.

"Here, take this," I said, handing one of my shabby brown blankets through the bars.

"Thank you, dear," she whispered. "I've been fighting a cold."

We sat for a few minutes, not saying anything even though I burned to ask her more. I finally got up the nerve and took a deep breath.

"Aggs…when do you get out of here?"

"I'm in for life," she replied grimly.

"*Life?*" I whispered incredulously. I certainly couldn't see this woman murdering someone, but no other crime deserved a life sentence. "Can I ask what happened?"

"I've been labeled a rogue because I openly rebelled against the Mainframe and their questionable practices."

"You?" I whispered. "But..."

"But you can't imagine it?" She replied, chuckling. "Most people can't because of my age, but until I got thrown in here, I advocated against the Mainframe's misinformation."

"What do you mean?"

"I mean, they've been ignoring the answer to our food problems for years. All you have to do to fix the soil is-"

"Grow plants that can handle the toxins," I finished. She nodded, tilting her head curiously as she stared at me.

"Why are you in here?"

"I'm not really in here for anything. I'm training in the military, but I ran away from the draft. They're taking me in to the Mainframe tomorrow."

Her eyes grew wide. "They didn't kill you?"

"They...need me." I hesitated. "It's a very long story."

"Oh." She lapsed into silence except for occasional coughing. Sitting still made me nervous and fidgety, so I scooted closer to the bars.

"So...how long have you been here, Aggs?"

"Just a couple years."

"Can't you appeal or something?"

She chuckled again. "Oh no, dear. The officials see me as a threat," she said. "And rightly so. If they want to imprison me for giving people information, then so be it."

"How did you fight against the government?"

"I know I may not look it, but in my younger days I reported for the news. I had quite a bit of influence in the city, and I tried to raise awareness about food and the effects of the Akrium testing with my columns, but no one listened. I lost my job and got sent up to the Mainframe for the trial. They branded me crazy and threw me in jail because they knew I was on to them."

For a moment, I wondered if she really might be crazy, but I'd become far too interested to stop talking now.

"You know about the Akrium testing?"

Aggs looked around and motioned me closer to the bars until we sat face to face.

"The others don't like to hear about the old stories. They say I should just shut my mouth and try to get out on good behavior."

"You mean about the mutations?"

"Yes…how do you know?" She cocked her head again.

"I…that's a long story too." She frowned a little, probably sensing my hesitation. "So you mean the stories are real? People mutated and became beasts?"

"Yes." Her face looked serious and pale in the dim light. I'd been able to dismiss the idea more easily when I thought only mom believed it, but now this strange woman knew about the beasts too.

"How do you know about the beasts?"

"The discovery of Akrium happened when I'd been a reporter for twenty years, but I happened to interview someone who'd been on the inside when the testing began. He told me about how things went wrong."

"My mom said they went into hiding."

"Yes, they did. They live in the southern forest. People used to call it the Shadowlands until people decided that the beasts just disappeared or weren't a threat anymore."

"Why do people think they disappeared?"

"Lots of people, especially in the Mainframe, thought that they might try to get revenge somehow, but so far nothing's happened. Only some odd disappearances, but in a city like this you learn not to get too worked up about things like that."

I leaned against the bars, deep in thought. Nothing made much sense. The beasts wouldn't just go peacefully live in the woods.

"But wait," I said suddenly as a memory flashed across my mind, "what about the weapons raid?"

"The what?"

"Didn't you hear? Someone invaded the Mainframe and stole a bunch of weapons."

She shrugged. "Yeah, but the Mainframe determined the criminals were draft defectors trying to get out of going to war."

"No, that's not right," I whispered, more to myself than Aggs. "They were in the city, they…"

Then everything clicked suddenly in my mind. "The beasts…they did it! They're planning something!"

"What do you mean?" Her eyes grew serious in the dim light.

"The beasts, I've seen them in the city. They found a way to disguise themselves, they're planning something. I…I don't know how to explain it, I just know."

She sat back and rubbed her chin. "I've wondered for a long time if they've been biding their time. Maybe you're right, and they're up to something big. Maybe this break-in was just the first step."

I felt an uneasy twinge in my stomach. Aggs rubbed her eyes tiredly and stared at the floor.

"My brother worked in the Defense Department, you know," she said suddenly. "They tested him, and when it failed, he left to join the beasts. I went to the Shadowlands and tried to free him, but as soon as he started making attempts to get out, the beasts killed him. That's when I gave up and tried to raise awareness about both the beasts and our food situation. Obviously, it didn't work. If anything, the beasts have made more headway into the Mainframe."

"Wait…you're saying they've infiltrated the Mainframe?"

"Of course! It makes sense, especially with your theory about the break-in. They'd have to get people on the inside, wouldn't they? I think that's a lot of the reason the officials don't see sense, why they started this war. Maybe the beasts are trying to collapse the Mainframe from the inside."

"Do you think they know they're being influenced?" I asked.

"I'm sure some are aware, but they're taken in to the point where they'll do anything they're told. Either that, or they're being threatened."

I stared down at the floor, trying to take in all this new information. Could I be sure of anything anymore? Maybe Aggs just spouted crazy talk, like everyone here seemed to think. But she acted so levelheaded, so knowledgeable.

I firmly pushed all the confusion from my mind, suddenly realizing how tired I felt. I tried to cover my yawn, but I couldn't.

"Poor dear. You're probably exhausted. Why don't you get some sleep?" Aggs smiled wanly through the bars.

"Wait, no, I really…" I stopped as I yawned again.

"Look, I would love to talk about it more, but you're about to fall asleep," she said with a grandmotherly sort of smile. "Get some sleep. You'll need it for tomorrow."

I nodded, feeling my eyelids droop. I wanted sleep so badly, but a huge part of me cowered in fear at the thought of morning. Aggs curled up on her small pallet near the bars and soon snored softly. I climbed onto my own, trying to calm my racing heart.

Chapter Thirty-Two

Someone shook me roughly awake the next morning. I opened my blurry eyes and looked up into the face of a surly guard. He leered at me unpleasantly and grabbed my arm.

He unlocked the gate and led me to the hall. Aggs stirred slightly and rolled over in her sleep. Without really knowing why, I said a silent prayer for her. Something about the way she crawled about her cell, looking as fragile as a porcelain doll, made my heart ache with pity.

We went through the long hall, prisoners rioting and shouting insults at me or the guard. Or both of us.

As we left the lobby and walked through the ominous iron doors, I saw a long black Mainframe car waited for us outside. A back door opened, and the guard shoved me roughly inside. The smooth leather felt weird under my hands after the straw-stuffed pallet in jail. I looked around warily and noticed Vic sitting by the far window, sipping some champagne.

"Well, nice of you to join us," he chuckled. "Care for some?"

He held up his small, bubbling goblet. I shook my head violently. Mom always disapproved of drinking. The memory caused a sharp pang of guilt and pain. I'd failed her. She'd put her own life on the line, lying for me, and it backfired. With a gut-wrenching flash of horror, I wondered if they'd try to look for her, since she'd helped me escape.

I stared silently down at my hands the whole ride. I wondered if things would have been different if I'd just stayed in my apartment, working quietly at the Ration Center. But then, mom wouldn't have been cured. She wouldn't be safe…or at least safer than she'd be in the city.

The car suddenly jerked to a stop. "What the…"

I looked up to see Vic mopping spilled champagne from his lap. "What's going on up there?"

"Beasts…everywhere!" shouted the driver.

"WHAT?" Vic suddenly looked like a lion, roaring in rage. Veins popped out of his meaty, red neck and his greasy hair flew around his sallow temples. "Where are they?"

He must have forgotten about me because he grabbed a huge gun from a hidden compartment and jumped out of the car. I ducked instinctively when I heard a series of rounds going off.

"Stay here!" I looked up and realized the driver shouted at me. He grabbed a pistol from another compartment and jumped out to join the fray. Timidly, I peeked through the window of the door where the driver left. Vic and the driver and someone else, some guard, shot at tons and tons of creatures flooding from every direction. My breath caught in my throat. Some looked sickeningly pale, almost a yellowish color, with no hair and red eyes. They laughed maniacally, shooting in every direction they could.

I cowered lower, unsure what to think. On the one hand, I hated Vic with a boiling passion, but on the other I didn't exactly want to help the beasts try to destroy him.

"We know you have the girl!" A voice, far beyond human, rasped loudly over the gunfire. "Give her to us! You owe us a cure!"

"Yeah, right, you really think I'm that stupid?" Vic's voice sounded a lot less greasy as he bellowed at the beasts.

Suddenly, a loud blast sounded and shook the car violently. I glanced out the other window and saw thousands of red eyes peering in at me. Icy fear clamped down on my heart, making my breath come in short gasps. I would be crushed. I had to get out of the car, but how? And how could I protect myself? I scrambled around, not knowing what to do. Vic and the driver found secreted guns, but it seemed like only they knew where the guns were hidden. Desperately, I groped around for a plastic edge or button. Finally, my fingers brushed some kind of edge. I tore at it with my nails until I opened up a small compartment in the back of a seat. I found a small black pistol waiting for me.

I picked it up with shaking hands. How would I know what to do? I'd never shot a gun before. I'd never needed to before.

Hesitantly, I pulled the trigger. A shot sounded, so loud that my ears rang for a few minutes.

I ducked to the door I'd looked out of just a second ago. Luckily, the beasts seemed to be on the other side of the car, trying to tip it over. I flung open the door and climbed out. Bullets flew over my head, pinging off the tough metal of the car. I scooted around the back, keeping the pistol pointed in the air with my finger on the trigger. As I rounded the far back corner, I saw several beasts tipping over the car while Vic and the others fired incessantly. More officers came out of the Mainframe building, firing guns and yelling.

"There she is!"

I turned toward the voice. My heart constricted with terror when I saw one of the red eyed monsters pointing straight at me. He turned and started running towards me. For a moment, everything seemed to slow down. A strange adrenaline spread through me, raising my hand for me, pointing the gun at the beast. I pulled the trigger. The loud shot rang out again, but it didn't affect my ears so much this time.

The beast flew back, black blood oozing from a huge hole in its shoulder. The other beasts and Mainframe workers gasped and stared. My mouth dropped in shock. Did he die? No...he just clutched his shoulder and got up. I hadn't killed him, but I dropped the gun, feeling sick. What had I just done?

Before I could get a grip or move or do something, someone dragged me to my feet with rough hands.

"All of you clear out! You've seen what she can do!"

Dimly, I looked down to see Vic's burly hands clutched around my arms. I looked up at him, a little bemused. Mainframe officers chased the beasts away. They all turned to look at me with those hideous red eyes as they fled. A couple more beasts got bullets to the chest or head, sending them flying.

"How did you know that?"

I turned back towards Vic. "Know what?"

"That beasts can be shot? That's their only vulnerability."

I opened my mouth uselessly a couple times. "I…I didn't."

Suddenly, a sickening grin spread over his face. "I knew it. Your eyes, they went all funny right before you shot him. You're just like them, but you're human enough not to become a barbarian. This is incredible. I knew I was right!"

He punched the air with his fist like he'd just won some kind of race. I stared at him in furious disbelief. Didn't he realize that I'd just seriously injured someone, that the memory of that beast flying back would haunt me for the rest of my life?

"Don't worry about him, Lily. He was a beast. Totally gone in the brain."

Vic still smiled. I couldn't *believe* this slimeball. He's part of the reason those people had become what they were. How could he just blow it off like that?

White hot anger spread through me, lighting my veins on fire. The same weird adrenaline that overcame before pulsed through me, giving me fresh power. I twisted my arm until I gripped Vic's arm in a vice-like hold. He screamed and winced in pain. I picked up my dropped gun and pointed it in his face.

"I'm not working for a disgusting, heartless flea-bag like you!" I hissed. My voice deepened to a growl. Everything felt unnatural and yet somehow familiar.

I have superhuman strength. I'm the only living hybrid, I thought, *the only one who can be both a beast and a normal human.* The fact spread through me, validating and scaring me at the same time.

Vic gasped, trying to raise his gun, but I knocked it out of his hand easily. In my peripheral, I saw other Mainframe officers rushing towards Vic, but I turned towards them. They stopped in unison, staring at me with horrified faces. A low, unearthly growl escaped me as I turned back to Vic.

"I'm not going to kill you," I hissed.

"Oh, thank you, thank you!" He groveled like a beggar, making me even more disgusted.

"I'm not a lowlife like you. Just meet my demands and I'll let you go."

His eyes grew wide as saucers. "What demands?" he choked.

"Bring Wes to me. Free him and end this stupid war. Then I'll let you go."

He gulped, sweat pouring down his forehead. "I...can't!"

I let go of his arm and grabbed his neck instead. "Why *not?*"

"He...he's already been deployed," he choked. "He's fighting in the southern province."

Chapter Thirty-Three

With a roar of rage and disgust, I threw Vic as hard as I could against the side of the car. The metal siding crumpled with the weight of the impact, shattering the glass in a few windows. Bullets flew around me, but I seemed to sense each one until one caught me in the leg. It didn't hurt much, but I still clutched my leg in pain.

"Grab her!"

A thousand people descended on me, their millions of hands raining down on my shoulders and head. They lifted me in the air, carried me on their upraised arms, a chaotic mob. They won. Vic won. I probably would have been safer with the beasts, even though I'd hurt one of them. No telling what would happen now.

In my mind, I saw a flash of white teeth, twinkling hazel eyes and curly brown hair.

"Wes," I whispered to myself. I would never see him again. I heard the clang of metal doors shutting, sealing me in my very own Mainframe tomb.

After what felt like hours, I woke up in a sterile white room. Everything around me shimmered immaculately. It felt so strange after the bloody scene on the streets. All my limbs felt like they'd been replaced with lead. I tried to move them, but they didn't budge. I panicked, moving and squirming as fast as I could until I discovered that leather straps held me down, two on each arm and leg and one around my stomach.

Finally, gasping for breath and covered in sweat, I laid back and tried to come up with a plan. Panic threatened to engulf me completely. I took a few deep breaths and felt my racing heart slow down a few notches. I tried flattening my arms against the hard plastic beneath me and sliding them out of the straps, but it didn't work. The straps held fast. I tried getting angry, but I only felt cold fear. My adrenaline would surely work against these straps, but I couldn't get it to come. Maybe I'd used all my power up.

I tried wiggling my legs next, but it didn't worked. The straps only seemed to get tighter. Frustrated, I clamped my hands open and shut and noticed a strange tickling sensation on my wrist.

I looked closer and saw that one of the belts had frayed slightly. The straps weren't made of leather after all, just some kind of cord.

How much time did I have? Were they watching me? What did it even matter? I rubbed my wrist furiously against the restraint. Some of the threads started to come loose when I heard a door open.

Vic limped into the room, his head heavily bandaged and his ankle in a plaster cast. He glared at me.

"So…thought you could do me in, eh?"

"No," I spat, trying to sound braver than I felt. "I'm not merciless like you."

"Well, you put on quite a show. You'll come in plenty useful after we fix you up a little."

My heart quickened its already frantic pace. "What do you mean?"

"We're going to wipe your memory. That way, all these pesky feelings won't get in the way and we'll be able to do our testing without fear of being maimed."

He spoke calmly, as if he were a doctor explaining the purpose of a shot.

"You're insane!" I screamed at him.

"No, I think that would be you. But we'll take care of that soon."

He smiled eerily. My anger came back, full and forceful.

Yes! I thought gleefully. I wrenched my arm up and the straps broke. I reached down and broke the other straps on my arm. After that, I kicked out as hard as I could and it busted the leg straps. Vic lunged at me with an angry growl before I could undo my stomach one, so I swung my leg as hard as I could at him. It made contact with Vic's already bandaged head, making a sickening thump. He dropped like a sack of potatoes. I worked quickly on the last strap, freeing myself at last.

I jumped off the table, surging with adrenaline. Miraculously, someone left my bag on the table beside the bed I'd been strapped to. I grabbed it and bent down to examine Vic. A small button lay by his hand. A panic button. I picked it up, along with a gun that fell out of a holster around his hip. I didn't know if he'd loaded it. I'd just have to take my chances.

I pushed the button and dropped it. Praying I wouldn't be seen, I ducked into the hall and scooted to the left. The right side ended in a blank wall. I found a stairwell just as thundering footsteps pounded into the room where I'd been confined.

Without waiting to hear their outraged yells, I ran down the maze-like stairway. It seemed to be some kind of Maintenance stairwell because it the railing looked shabby and gray unlike the pristine marble steps in the main offices. I finally came to two doors at the bottom of the staircase and breathed a sigh of relief. Through the window of one, I saw a side parking lot. The other led into the front lobby.

I noticed a red alarm over the outside door, but if anyone would hear me, it might as well be now. I pushed through the door, setting off a loud, blaring alarm and ran as fast as I could. My adrenaline didn't feel as strong as it before, but I could still run pretty far without getting winded. I made it to Front Street before I needed a break.

It suddenly struck me that I didn't have a plan. I couldn't stay in the city. Way too dangerous and I'd be found for sure. I could go to the beach, hide out there for a few days. Wes and I planned that before…

I pushed the thought firmly from my mind. I needed to concentrate, to escape fast, to get supplies. I only had a little food in my bag, left over from Deb's. I took a deep breath and started running again through the alleys to my apartment. I wrenched the door and found it open.

I barely had time to register that someone tore the place apart. The table and chairs lay overturned. The contents of the cupboards lay strewn across the old carpeting. A million flashbacks ran through my mind-the morning of the beach trip, mom's diagnosis, the summons…it all happened here. Who would come in and destroy everything, my memories? Even though the place wasn't much, mom and I made it our own. How could they?

I clenched my fists in fury, wanting to tear Vic limb from limb, but I couldn't get angry now. I groped around on the floor and grabbed a box of cereal and some granola bars and put them in my bag. After one last sad look around the apartment, I ran down the steps.

I'd never make it to the beach if I ran, but my truck would give me away in a second. But if I'd lasted this long I could last a little longer. As I jumped down from the last stair, I stopped short. Someone set up roadblocks in both directions.

I ducked down an alley and held my breath. Chaotic shouts and orders filled the air. I tried to figure out what direction they came from, but I couldn't make sense of it. Finally, I inched down the alley and out the other end. A few more alleys took me to Front street, where armed, uniformed guards patrolled, looking sour. How did they get out so fast?

Frantically, I scuttled like a rat to other alleyways farther down the road away from the officers.

I found the small outlet road to the beach and ran as fast as I could. In a few minutes, I'd reach the shore and safety. No one would find me there, for a while at least.

I hit the sand and kept running even though my lungs burned. I felt a sharp pang in my leg and looked down to see a bloody bandage wrapped around it. I hadn't noticed it before. Someone from the Mainframe bandaged and cleaned the bullet wound, but the pressure of running made it bleed heavily.

I pulled up short, terrified. How could I run like this? In my hurry, I hadn't even noticed the sun going down. How long had I laid on that creepy bed?

Suddenly, my blood froze like ice in my veins. A steady thrum sounded overhead, the thrum of helicopter blades. The helicopter waved a searchlight through the air, the circular rays of light scanning the pale sand.

They're looking for me, I thought fearfully. The thought scared me, but also gave me renewed strength. Hastily, I tightened the bandage, trying frantically to remember what I'd learned about first aid in school. I tested my leg, sure I could run on it a while longer. The searchlight flicked so close to me for a second that I held my breath and bit my lip to keep from screaming out.

I could run now, but where? No way could I go back to the city. I'd never make it trying to run farther inland. They'd find me on the beach.

And then, a grim realization settled in. I couldn't…could I? But no matter how I looked at it, no matter how I analyzed the situation, I always came to the same conclusion. I had nowhere to go but the Shadowlands.

Chapter Thirty-Four

With my last bit of strength, I ran pell-mell towards the trees, praying the helicopter wouldn't see me. Flashes of light flickered around me, over my head. I heard stern shouts, felt handcuffs on my wrists...*I'm hallucinating.* I pushed on, giving myself landmarks to run to. That huge boulder, the scrubby oak behind the sand line, the massive pine towering over my head.

Soon, a rising crescent moon lit a path for me on the forest floor. An eerie mist began to rise from the ground, making my terror peak.

When the pain in my leg finally became unbearable, I scrambled to the shadow of a thick tree and knelt in the pine needles, gasping for breath. A sheet of sweat covered me all over, making my hair stick to my forehead and neck. I glanced down at the bullet wound and looked away quickly, trying to hold in my nausea. Blood poured again from the wound. The wrapping must have fallen off. I couldn't see it anywhere. Desperately, I tore the bottom of my shirt off and wrapped it quickly above and around the wound. The blood flow tapered a little, but not much.

After my breathing slowed, I realized I couldn't hear anything. I strained my ears, I couldn't hear even the faint beat of helicopter blades. I let out a shaky sigh of relief, but my respite soon gave way to terror. The trees, the mist, the moonlight...it looked just like the nightmare I'd had the night Wes had brought me home from the hospital. Panic threatened to overwhelm me.

A new horror crept over me as I realized just how dire things had become. I sat hunched by a tree in a forest full of man-eating mutants with a bum leg. A bum leg that could get infected. I took some deep breaths and tried to just be grateful I hadn't been caught.

"I'll eat something," I said to no one in particular. "Then I'll feel better."

I opened my bag and rummaged around for a granola bar, but stopped when I saw the bouquet of flowers Wes gave me for my birthday. They'd withered and dried, but still looked beautiful. A tear slipped down my cheek. Most of the flowers had large heads with petals that stretched wide open like a yawning mouth, but a few were long with small bunches of purple at the ends. Heather, the stuff Deb grew in her garden. The plant that cleansed the soil. I hugged the flowers close to me, clinging to the memory of that perfect sunny beach up north.

"I'll find you, Wes," I whispered. "Don't worry."

The words slightly reassured me. Wes wouldn't give up and neither would I.

With a pang of sadness, I laid back on the soft pine needles and hugged my knees to my chest, my hunger forgotten. Things looked bad, but they could always be worse. I'd escaped Vic. I might have a chance to escape to the Southern Province and find Wes. I had hope.

With these comforting thoughts, I scooted closer to the tree, trying to ignore the sharp pain in my leg. For now, I would be safe.

Brittiany West is the author of several short stories, a novella and two novels. She began her writing career as a reporter and columnist for a small town newspaper. The Shadowlands Series are her breakout novels. Mrs. West lives in Ohio with her husband and five children.

Printed in Great Britain
by Amazon.co.uk, Ltd.,
Marston Gate.